The young widow Isobel Carnegie is much sought after for her beauty as well as her fortune. But when she is kidnapped by the Highland chieftain Hector MacLean it seems that he is only interested in her money.

The gently-bred Isobel is horrified by the hard life led by the clansmen at Ardshee and when Hector is called to join the forces of Bonnie Prince Charlie she seizes her chance of escape.

It is only when she meets up again with her once-proud husband, now weary and broken-hearted by the loss of his clan on the bleak battlefield of Culloden, that Isobel realises where her heart truly lies.

GW00356675

The Chieftain
Caroline Martin

MILLS & BOON LIMITED
London · Sydney · Toronto

First published in Great Britain 1982
by Mills & Boon Limited, 15–16 Brook's Mews,
London W1A 1DR

© Caroline Martin 1982
Australian copyright 1982
Philippine copyright 1982

ISBN 0 263 73906 6

04/0782/

Set in 10 on 10 pt Linotron Times

Photoset by Rowland Phototypesetting Ltd
Bury St Edmunds, Suffolk
Made and printed in Great Britain by
Cox & Wyman Ltd, Reading

CHAPTER ONE

'THIS time,' said Isobel Carnegie, eight days after her husband's funeral, 'this time I shall marry to please myself.'

She spoke quietly, in her usual low musical tones, but with an unmistakable emphasis. Her father, standing beside her in the sunlit garden, glanced sharply round, and was almost surprised to find that her expression was as tranquil and gentle as ever.

She smiled slightly, and went on: 'But I know I must not be hasty. I want to be sure I make the right choice.'

Her father took her hand and slid it under his arm, patting it consolingly.

'No one would deny you've earned yourself the right to choose, my girl.'

They walked on slowly, along the neat grass path between the riotously blooming roses, silent again, their thoughts very far from the summertime beauty around them. They were thinking instead of a darkened, over-heated room, of a tall figure motionless on the curtained bed, of the two years of Isobel's life which had been spent in ceaseless attendance on the man who was her husband only in name. She was nineteen now, and two years of her girlhood had passed without joy or light-heartedness. 'Yes,' thought Andrew Reid, his hand over hers; 'Isobel has earned the right to a little happiness, now it is all over—'

They were still walking together in companionable silence when Isobel's mother brought John Campbell out to the garden to join them. As he came forward, hand outstretched, Isobel greeted him with transparent pleasure and the warmth due to a long-established friend. Every inch the prosperous lawyer, from his neat

wig to his gleaming buckled shoes, John Campbell had
given her his support and comfort and sensible advice
throughout the long months of her husband's illness.
Now, when she thought of marrying again, some instinct
told her that she could do worse than take John Campbell—and that in his quiet way he cared very deeply for
her.

She put her hand in his and smiled sweetly up at him
with all the girlish innocence she had never lost.

'I was beginning to think you'd abandoned us, Mr
Campbell,' she said. 'We've not seen you since—' She
broke off, and he pressed her hand sympathetically.

'I felt sure that you would have most need of your
family about you at this time, Mrs Carnegie,' he said. 'I
know you must feel more relief than sorrow, in the
circumstances, but still—James Carnegie was a good
man, though you never knew him in his prime.'

'No,' she agreed. 'I did not meet him until a short
while before we were married, and he was so ill.'

'You can comfort yourself with the thought that your
devotion must greatly have eased his last years,' John
Campbell assured her. 'And you are young still—'

She raised her eyes to his face, searching for a clue to
his feelings. Was he about to declare the affection she
had long suspected lay hidden behind that courteous
manner? But he smiled suddenly, and patted her hand,
and moved on to remark upon the fine weather. And
before long he was deep in discussion with her father on
the politics of the day.

They had reached the subject of the Young Pretender
when Isobel grew tired and wandered off alone towards
the orchard at the far end of the garden. She knew how
the talk would go now, in endless speculation as to
whether or not the Young Pretender, Prince Charles
Edward Stuart, was likely to cross the sea to Scotland
and make a bid for the throne now securely held by King
George II.

Instinctively, Isobel's eyes were drawn at the thought
to that distant point beyond the garden wall, far across
the ripening fields of corn, where a broken jagged ridge

of mountains, purple blue, marked the Highland line. From those mountains, thirty years ago, men had come in support of the Old Pretender: wild barbarians of strange speech and uncouth dress, fierce and uncivilized and terrifying. She shivered now, remembering the tales she had heard. And then she comforted herself with the thought that the Jacobite rising of 1715 had failed dismally, and there was no reason to believe it could ever happen again. In any case, John Campbell was a Highlander by birth, though long settled in the Lowlands, and there was nothing frightening about him: times had changed. She looked around the orderly garden, and felt calm again.

A low wall bordered the orchard, and she sat on it, noting the ripening apples—small still, but growing— and the forget-me-nots under the trees. A little breeze stirred the long grass and brushed lightly against her, and she closed her eyes in contentment: it was good to be alone, and free, and in the open air after so long indoors.

It was the sound of a gate opening which disturbed her: the gate which led through the orchard wall into the road beyond. She glanced round sharply, and then rose to her feet in alarm.

For an instant she thought her fears of a moment ago had taken shape there in the dappled light beneath the trees. But that was foolish, and she told herself so, though she drew back behind the doubtful protection of the little wall and tried to hide her dismay.

The man in the orchard moved nearer, a wild dark figure in trews and jacket and plaid as brightly coloured as the green trees with their rosy apples. Isobel repressed an urge to scream and drew herself, trembling a little, to her full height—which was tall for a woman.

'What are you doing here?' she demanded, her voice shaking in spite of her efforts to control it.

To her astonishment the man removed his blue bonnet and bowed, with undeniable courtliness, and then stood gazing at her for a moment in silence. A slight smile curved his wide supple mouth.

'MacLean of Ardshee, at your service,' he said, by way of introduction. 'I believe this is the residence of Mrs Carnegie? I seek the favour of a word or two with her.'

His voice was deep and resonant, with more of a lilt than an accent, unlike the distinctively Scots speech of her family and friends. In spite of herself, she acknowledged that it had an attractive musical sound. Then she realised what he was asking, and after a moment's hesitation said cautiously: 'I am Mrs Carnegie.'

She watched his eyes widen with transparent amazement and coloured a little, wondering what was so surprising about her appearance. They were very dark eyes, she observed, long lashed and glowing with an emotion which set her cheeks burning the more. She ceased to notice the alarming tartan, and saw instead that he was young—not much older than herself she thought—and about her own height, and slender, with a lithe cat-like grace of movement. His lean oval face was deeply tanned, his thick black hair springing in curls which the ribbon at the nape of his neck could scarcely confine. There was a long pause as they gazed at one another.

Isobel felt very strange: she had never felt so odd before, with that lurching sensation in the pit of her stomach and that disquieting breathlessness. It was quite a different emotion from the fear of a moment ago, and entirely new to her.

The young man bowed again, more deeply this time. 'Then I am the more at your service, madam,' he said. 'In fact I would beg to lay myself and all I have at your feet, to your use for ever.'

She looked at him in bewilderment.

'Forgive me, but I do not quite understand, Mr . . . Mr MacLean.'

He placed one hand over his heart, though his eyes held a mocking sparkle of laughter, as if he were not wholly serious. 'I am asking, Mrs Carnegie, for your hand in marriage.'

Isobel gasped, and reached out to support herself on

the wall. What answer she would have given then she was never to know, for she heard footsteps coming along the path behind her, and John Campbell's voice broke in, sharp with astonishment.

'Ardshee!'

She glanced round. She had never before seen John look like that, with an expression mingling amazement and anger and something rather more unpleasant. He knew the intruder then, and did not like him.

She turned back to the man under the trees and saw that he too had lost all trace of the easy good manners of before. His eyes smouldered, black as coals beneath the straight brows, and for a moment his slender fingers hovered over the handle of the dirk he wore thrust into his belt. Then with a conscious effort he relaxed and let his hands fall to his side, though Isobel had the feeling that this was the stillness of a wild animal, alert and on its guard, ready to spring into action in an instant. When he spoke again his voice was very soft, but it had a dangerous edge.

'John Campbell! So you are here before me! I might have known.'

John gave a muffled exclamation, and pulled Isobel back to stand behind him.

'You insult me, sir!' he retorted. 'I have known Mrs Carnegie for many years, and her late husband before her. I am no fortune hunter.'

Isobel saw the colour leap to the young Highlander's cheeks, as he bit his lip to keep back the angry retort. When he did speak it was in Gaelic, softly, the words carefully measured. Isobel had never heard Gaelic spoken before, and she did not understand a word, but she was quite certain from the tone and the glint in the speaker's eyes that every lilting phrase held a well-chosen insult.

But if that was the intention, the words missed their target completely. John Campbell gazed blankly back at the younger man, as uncomprehending as Isobel. He gave a forced laugh, and said lightly:

'I would ask you to speak in English before the lady. It

is the only fit language for civilised ears. You insult her by your words, sir.'

'On the contrary, John Campbell, the insult was intended for you,' returned the Highlander smoothly. 'I said nothing fit for a lady's hearing. But it would seem you have long forgotten your birth and the language of your people. You have become a creature without a name or a heritage.'

John was crimson now to the ears, his blue eyes bright with rage.

'Thank God at least I have not your name! Thief, and murderer—!'

The blade of the Highlander's dirk flashed brilliantly in the sunlight as he leapt forward. Isobel screamed in terror, and threw herself in his path; John struggled to pull her aside; the Highlander paused: and Andrew Reid and his wife came running along the path towards them.

'What in heaven's name is all this?' demanded Isobel's father, glancing swiftly from one to another of the angry and frightened faces about him. 'You—' A contemptuous glance swept the Highlander. 'What are you doing here?'

In a moment the dirk was sheathed, the furious young man restored to his former courtliness as he bent in a sweeping bow.

'I am MacLean of Ardshee, with one hundred fighting men to my name,' he replied proudly, though there was a dangerous light lingering still somewhere in his eyes. 'I come to seek the hand of Mrs Carnegie in marriage.'

'Marriage!' It was Andrew Reid's turn now to explode in fury. 'She has been scarcely widowed a week! How can you insult her so?'

Isobel thought that for a moment the young man looked almost disconcerted, but he answered quietly enough.

'I understand that it was—' he paused, seeking the most tactful words, and went on: 'scarcely a marriage, shall we say.'

'Get out!' Andrew Reid broke in. 'You have said more than enough! Get out, and do not dare to show your face here again. You insult my daughter beyond endurance!'

The Highlander drew himself up to his full height, his head held with arrogant poise.

'I leave only at Mrs Carnegie's express request,' he returned haughtily. His eyes met Isobel's, level and expressionless. The emotions she felt now were also a little foreign to her, but she recognised them at once: anger, and disgust, and a feeling that he had somehow dirtied her by the naked greed of his proposal.

'Then I do request it,' she said, the coldness of her tone matching his, though there was a quiver of anger in it too. 'Most strongly,' she added with emphasis. 'You will leave us at once.'

His eyes darted a look of intense hatred in her direction, and then he bowed stiffly, his mouth set in a harsh line.

'Good day, Mrs Carnegie,' he said, 'and to you—and you—' He bent his head towards her parents, deliberately excluding John Campbell.

Then he turned sharply on his heel and in a final swirl of tartan left the garden.

With satisfaction and relief Isobel saw the gate close behind him. But as she turned to take her father's arm she had an odd sense that something vibrantly alive, some promise of excitement and adventure, had gone with their unwanted guest. Everyone around her seemed to have become suddenly curiously flat and dull, from John Campbell in his powdered wig and snuff-coloured coat, to her mother in her grey silk. Even the roses looked faded.

They walked slowly together towards the house, regaining their customary composed good manners with each step.

'Who is that objectionable young man?' Andrew Reid asked as they went. 'You seemed to be acquainted with him.'

'Yes,' admitted John Campbell, with a glance at Isobel. 'It is a long story, and one scarcely fit for a lady's ears. Suffice it to say that Hector MacLean is the penniless chieftain of an insignificant clan, and the latest in a long line of thieves and scoundrels.'

'You called him a murderer,' Isobel reminded him.

John halted, frowning slightly; and after a moment he said: 'Yes, Mrs Carnegie. And I fear I did not use the word lightly.' There was another pause, and then his voice fell so that they could scarcely hear him. 'But it was because of his father I used the word. And in memory of my father whom Alan MacLean killed in furtherance of a cattle raid, when I was still a child. For that, though I would not take the Highland way of revenge, I can never forgive, nor forget.'

Impulsively, Isobel took his hand in hers, her eyes warm with sympathy.

'Then I am glad indeed that I sent him away—and only sorry I did not do it before you came on the scene, to have such terrible memories brought to mind.'

'Thank you for that,' he said, huskily. 'For my part I regret deeply that you were subjected to so insulting an offer. There can, I fear, be no doubt of his motives. Though how he dared to come like that, so soon—' Words failed him, and he broke off.

Andrew Reid drew Isobel closer to him.

'We must make sure that in future no such rogue comes near her,' he said firmly. 'We who love her must keep her safe from insults of that kind, at all costs.'

'Most certainly,' agreed John, with decision. 'And you know you will have my assistance in that, to the limits of my power.'

CHAPTER
TWO

HECTOR MacLean might be the first suitor to be attracted
to Isobel by her late husband's great wealth, but he was
certainly not the last. In fact two more chance callers
were at the door on the very next day, and after that the
flow of eager visitors never ceased. Few were as open
about their intentions as Hector. Some came to inquire
after the young widow's health, a little embarrassed by
the fact that they scarcely knew her; others pretended to
long acquaintance or a distant family relationship to gain
access to her. But in fact Isobel saw none of them. With
her agreement, her father turned the most ineligible
from the door, and her mother received the more pre-
sentable in the parlour and entertained them politely
over tea and cakes. But all went away disappointed.

Only John Campbell was admitted freely to see
Isobel, and more and more she came to value his quiet
manners, his air of strength and good sense. For two
years of her life she had borne single-handed all the
burdens of caring for a man she did not love and scarcely
knew; now the thought of being protected and cherished
and cared for was very appealing. But she must give it a
little more time, and make quite sure that she wanted to
share her life with him. She understood so little of what
marriage meant, and there was no need to hurry. Meanwhile she walked in the garden with John at her side, and
told him her feelings, and enjoyed his kindly, loving
attentiveness.

It was her father who had all the anxieties to face. It
was he who had a bolt attached to the garden door, and
made sure she went nowhere unattended, and dealt with
the troublesome suitors. And he knew very well that it
was not simply her fortune and her beauty which

attracted these men, but also the fact that Isobel the
widow was a virgin still, untouched and unawakened. It
was very well known that James Carnegie had suffered
an apoplectic fit on the afternoon of their wedding day
and lain speechless and paralysed ever after. Most of the
men who flocked to the door had been waiting eagerly
for the past two years, expecting every hour to hear of
James Carnegie's death. That it had not come sooner
was, Andrew knew, due largely to Isobel's devoted care.

'I think,' he said proudly to John one day, 'there's not
another girl in Scotland who'd have kept her marriage
vows so faithfully with no hope of anything in return.
And it's not as if he had very much to offer before he was
ill—a fortune, of course, and he was a kindly man—but
old enough to be her father, and with no good looks to
speak of—' He sighed. 'Many times I've wished we'd
never urged the match on her, but there—we can't know
what's to come.'

'And perhaps she's the better for it,' John consoled
him. 'For was she not a little wilful in her younger days?
The past years have calmed and matured her. I watched
her grow up through the months of her married life. The
man who wins her now will be fortunate indeed.'

Andrew Reid looked at him thoughtfully.

'Aye, very fortunate, my friend. And he'll have to be
something of a hero to be worthy of my girl.' He saw
John's face fall, and smiled kindly. 'We'll see—we'll
see—' he said.

'He's a fair few years older than Isobel,' he was
thinking, 'and no more good looking than James Carnegie; but a good man, making a name for himself in his
quiet way—and he cares for her, that's plain. If she
should want him, she could do worse. Time will tell.'

His greatest pleasure these days lay in watching the
colour return to his daughter's cheeks, and the pretty
girlish roundness which months of sleeplessness and
constant anxiety had worn away. He thought proudly
that she was like the summer countryside itself, with that
complexion of honey and rose, those eyes blue as the
morning sky, that silken hair the colour of ripened corn:

lovelier far than her mother in her younger days, though she too had been a beauty once.

As the days passed Isobel began to feel as if she were slowly awakening from a bad dream. The past two years became gradually a merciful blur in her memory, and she began instead to remember her life before her marriage, the simple pleasures of family life, the walks and picnics, the laughter and games. But those things seemed to have gone for ever, and she had not yet found whatever pleasures life now had to offer. Sometimes, now and then, she felt a yearning restlessness, an uneasy longing for something unknown and unrecognised. She was not bored, but she felt all the same that something was missing.

It rained heavily one Sunday morning about three weeks after the funeral, and Isobel agreed to have her coach brought to the door to convey herself, her parents, and her maid, Janet, to the Kirk for the morning service.

'I'm beginning to fear we're haunted by Highlanders,' exclaimed her mother, as her father gave the coachman his orders to move.

'Oh?' enquired Isobel. The memory of the Highlander in the garden still had power to bring the colour to her cheeks. 'Why is that?'

'There's another one skulking out there just now, looking as if he's up to no good. Did I not tell you of the man who was gazing into the window of Widow Frazer's shop last Wednesday forenoon? Very odd, for I can't imagine he had need of ribbons and laces—soap perhaps, by the smell of him, but that's another story. They seem to be popping up all over the place wherever I go. I do hope it doesn't bode ill for us, with all these rumours of that tiresome young man across the water—'

'Och, come now, Margaret my dear, surely to goodness a man can do his shopping in town without giving cause to think the Pretender's upon us? Maybe he wanted some knick knack for his sweetheart back home. After all, they are but men, if barbarous in dress and

behaviour. Clean them and dress them like ourselves
and teach them English and give them some education,
and you'd scarcely be able to tell the difference. Take
John Campbell, for instance—'

'Oh, John's quite another matter—and he has passed
most of his life among us. I don't think he'd wish to call
himself a Highlander now. He would agree with us on
that score. No, John now, he's—' Isobel was glad to
listen to the ensuing discussion of John's virtues, until
the church was reached.

The service was long and the sermon impassioned,
and when they emerged at last into the fresh air the rain
had long since given way to brilliant sunshine. Isobel
would dearly have loved to walk home, but her father
bundled them into the coach saying it was already long
past dinner time, and they set off down the street for
home.

A little further on the coach rounded a corner and
then lurched suddenly, and drew to a shuddering halt.

Andrew Reid put his head out of the window and
called to the coachman. After a moment or two of a
shouted exchange he drew back and said quickly:

'There's been an accident ahead—some old woman
hurt, he thinks. I'll go and see—wait here.'

He scrambled out, closing the door behind him, and
disappeared from view.

'Poor old soul!' murmured Isobel. 'Do you think we
should go and help?'

'Your father will let us know if there's anything we can
do,' her mother reassured her.

They waited quietly, talking of nothing in particular,
and a few minutes passed. And then all of a sudden the
coach quivered, jolted, and started forward at an alarming speed.

Eyes wide, Isobel clung to the door, crying: 'Oh,
mother, the old woman! Oh, what can he be thinking
of?'

And then she caught one fleeting glimpse of her
father, white-faced, horrified, pinned to one side by two
rough tartan-clad figures, while behind them a third held

a knife to the coachman's throat. Her hand flew to her mouth.

'Oh dear God, who is driving? What's happened?'

Her mother screamed, and flew to the door, trying to force it open. Isobel grasped her.

'No, no! You'll be killed at this speed. Oh, sit still, mother dear—Janet, help me!'

Together they pulled Mrs Reid to safety, and she subsided onto the seat, sobbing wildly.

'Oh, it's the Highlanders, I know it is! We shall all be murdered in our beds!'

'Nonsense,' said Isobel as calmly as she could, but hoping her mother had not seen who had her father prisoner. 'And we're not in our beds.'

It was doubtful comfort, and had little effect on Margaret Reid. So distraught was she that it was not for some time that Isobel realised they had left the town and were travelling fast through the countryside. It was not a reassuring sight, but she did not risk speaking of it.

'What has happened?' she thought. 'Who can be doing this, and why? Or have the horses simply bolted?' But she knew that was unlikely, or the coach would not have kept so unerringly to the road for so long.

And then at last, in the cool shade of a wood, the coach turned into a narrow lane and halted. Orders were shouted, there was a distant noise of horses' hooves, over and above the coach horses, and then all at once the door was flung open. Hands reached in, and Isobel felt herself grasped and dragged roughly into the open.

Then, horribly, the door was slammed shut again, an order shouted in Gaelic, and the coach drove on, out of her sight.

'Mother!' she cried in agony, and tried desperately to run along the lane after it.

'She'll be safe enough. He'll leave the coach at the next crossroads. They'll have a long walk home, but they'll take no harm.'

She knew that voice, deep and lilting, completely untroubled. She turned sharply and met those unforgettable dark eyes, full of ironic amusement. Hector MacLean bowed.

'We meet again, Mrs Carnegie. I give you that name,' he added, 'because it is still yours. But not for long . . . I do not like to be insulted.'

She felt the fear trickle coldly down her spine. Did he mean to murder her then?

'What . . . what do you mean?' she whispered through dry lips.

'You'll know soon enough.' He called another order in Gaelic, more softly this time, and she saw that the wood seemed to be crowded with Highlanders, and that it was not horses she had heard, but ponies, the shaggy sure-footed garrons best suited to the mountains. One was brought forward, and she realised she was supposed to mount. White with fear though she was she shook her head. Hector MacLean drew his dirk.

'Do you want me to bind you to the beast? Get up.'

She could not argue with the gleaming blade, and struggled onto the pony's broad back, with a little ungentle assistance from Hector. And then most of the others mounted, bareback like herself, and they set off into the trees, one man leading her pony. They went quickly, but the men on foot kept pace with them easily, moving with silent loping strides through the patchwork of light and shadow. She noticed how the bright tartan merged into the background as they went, and understood its advantages as clothing for a race of cattle thieves and murderers. Was she to be their latest victim?

She was too frightened to take much notice of where they were going. In any case it was all unfamiliar to her. She was aware only that after a time they left the wood and emerged into the bright hot sunlight, and then that they splashed through a shallow burn. On through another wood, and then along the edge of a cornfield, and a second, until at last they came to a cottage sheltered by trees and halted in the ivy-shaded yard behind it.

The cottage looked almost derelict, with holes in the

roof and broken windows: it could not have been lived in for years. But it was not empty now. Yet more Highlanders came softly out to greet them, speaking quietly in Gaelic, but clearly excited. Innumerable pairs of eyes peered up at her, full of lively interest from beneath shaggy fringes of hair. She shuddered, and recoiled as one man reached out a grimy hand to finger the shining black silk of her gown. But at a sharp command from Hector he retreated at once.

It was the only kindness she was likely to receive from her captor, she knew that: and sure enough he slid his dirk once more from his belt and turned to her, saying coldly:

'Into the house with you, Mrs Carnegie.'

There was no point in arguing. She was quite sure that any defiance on her part would result in Hector letting loose that wild-looking mob upon her, to do their worst. She walked obediently, with a sleepwalker's dazed half-consciousness, towards the back door of the cottage, half off its rusted hinges.

There was an evil-smelling kitchen, and beyond that a living room, lit with a dim green light because of the trees and bushes which crowded close to its windows. And in there waited a small, respectable looking man, dressed in tidy dark grey, with brown hair neatly tied back, and a small leather-bound book in his hand. He came forward as if to greet her, but paused as Hector spoke to him in Gaelic.

Then she realised that Hector had bent close to her and was whispering into her ear.

'One little sign that you're less than willing, and you'll not see the moon rise tonight,' he warned.

She gazed at him in bewilderment, and then back at the other man, and then at the three Highlanders who had followed them into the room, closing the door behind them. Her heart beat fast with terror. What was going to happen now?

Then Hector took her left hand in his, and led her forward to stand before the quiet man, who cleared his throat, and opened his book, and began to read. And

Isobel realised with appalling clarity that Hector Mac-Lean had brought her here to make her his wife.

In panic she glanced wide-eyed about her, but she knew there was no escape. It would be easy enough to conceal a body in this deserted and lonely spot, and then no one might ever know what had become of her. She realised that the minister—if such he was—had paused, and was looking at her with concern, and she turned back quickly to face him, trying to appear as calm and untroubled as possible. If only her hands did not tremble so! But perhaps he would think it natural for a fugitive bride to be nervous. What tale, she wondered, had Hector told him? That they must marry secretly, as they loved in spite of her family's disapproval?

Then she wondered about the minister. Was he indeed a minister of the Scottish Kirk? Or was he perhaps a Catholic priest, or a non-juring episcopal clergyman in trouble for refusing the oath of allegiance to the King? She knew many Highlanders preferred these forbidden faiths to the Presbyterian church of the land. Would this marriage be legal if he were not a minister? She could not guess from the words he read: though the service was conducted in English she was too frightened to remember if her first marriage had followed the same form.

But she was careful all the same to give the right answers, as clearly as she could, though her voice was low and shaking. She did not look up once, not even when she felt Hector raise her hand to push his ring onto the finger where James Carnegie's had once lain. She realised he must have removed that some time before the ceremony, but she did not remember him doing so.

And then his hands grasped her shoulders, and she felt his lips cool and light on her forehead, and she knew it was over.

She raised her eyes to his face, and saw that he had already turned away to thank the minister and share his satisfaction with the other men. That more than anything else told her with chilling certainty how cold-blooded was his choice of her to be his wife. She bit her lip sharply to keep back the tears, for she must not weep yet, not until she was alone.

If ever she were to be alone again. For she realised she had no idea what would happen, now she had been bound before God to this frightening stranger. Would Hector take her with him to his home, wherever it was? Or let her go back to her parents, now she bore his name, and come to claim the fortune he had stolen with her? 'Please let him do that,' she thought, but without hope.

They were passing a leather bottle round now, laughing and joking in Gaelic, never once looking at her. The minister had joined them, and seemed to be in as convivial a mood as the rest of them.

She wondered fleetingly if they would notice if she crept to the window and tried to escape, but she knew she would attract attention trying to break enough of that jagged glass to climb through. Was there any other way out?

She jumped as a hand grasped her elbow. Hector was at her side, his eyes very dark, close to her face.

'Upstairs now, Mrs MacLean,' he said softly.

She followed his gaze then to a shadowy corner of the room, where a rickety ladder led up into darkness. She could scarcely breathe for the frantic beating of her heart. She tried to obey his commanding pressure on her elbow, but her limbs seemed to have lost all power to move. For a moment he whispered menacingly in her ear, and tried to urge her on, and then he laughed sharply—and unpleasantly—and swept her off her feet into his arms.

There was a great encouraging shout of laughter from his companions, and they called after him as he bore her across the room to the ladder and mounted it slowly, sure-footed as a cat on the narrow rungs. She was half-fainting now, limp in his arms.

At the top of the ladder was an attic running the length of the cottage, lit only by holes where the thatch had fallen from the roof. It was cleaner than the rooms downstairs, and a heap of dried heather had been spread at one side, covered with a plaid.

'Brought from Ardshee for our marriage bed,' he explained in a whisper. And there, on that makeshift bed, he laid her down.

She stirred and tried to rise.

'No!' she moaned piteously, but he was unmoved. He stood looking down at her, his hands busy laying aside the dirk and unbuckling his belt.

'No one,' he said softly, 'will ever be able to say that I am your husband in name only.'

She slid onto her knees and clasped his feet, light and slender in the deerskin brogues, and gazed imploringly up at him.

'Please! Please, I beg you, let me go home!' She kept her voice low, choking with tears, and wondered if he heard her through the growing din downstairs: they were singing now.

But if he had heard her the grief in her voice did not touch his heart, for he bent and thrust her roughly back on the bed, and then his mouth came fiercely down on hers, hard, relentless, demanding.

She tried to struggle, but his lean strong body held her pinioned, while his hands moved over her, tugging at the lacing of her bodice, undressing her with neat-fingered efficiency. She felt him pull the dark silk from her body and then the petticoats and the rest of her clothes until at last she lay naked and defenceless. And only then did he draw back to look at her. Breathless and trembling with terror she watched him, and saw how his eyes were narrowed with emotion, his expression grave but unreadable. There was a little pause, and then he whispered suddenly:

'*Dhia*, Isobel MacLean, but you are beautiful!'

The depth of passion in his words sent a strange vibration coursing through her, and she seemed to see him for the first time today without that blinding haze of fear. It was almost as if she felt rather than saw the fine-boned face, the glowing eyes, the thickly waving hair, the beautiful hands; the lean supple body emphasised by the close fitting trews and the graceful folds of the plaid. A long shuddering tremor shook her, though it had nothing to do with the terror of a moment ago, and she closed her eyes against the force of that new dizzying sensation.

But she knew all the same when he fell on his knees at her side, aware of his closeness before he came to her. And she knew this was not the Hector of before, but a man moved by the same power that held her, so that his touch was gentle in its urgency, his mouth warm with desire as it met hers.

Slowly, inexorably, the last faint traces of fear left her, and an aching sweetness possessed her and woke her to life as his arms closed about her. Against all the impulses of her heart and mind and will she gave herself to him and surrendered to the need which had lain waiting in her through the long lonely years.

And then all at once it was over, and as she opened eyes dazed with delight she saw that the ardent lover of those exquisite moments had gone as if he had never been. He had what he wanted, and now her usefulness was at an end. He drew away from her and sprang to his feet, pulling his belt about him and adjusting his plaid, his dark face a cool mask of indifference.

'Get dressed,' he ordered curtly. 'We've a long way to go. Come as soon as you're ready.' And he walked briskly away and disappeared down the ladder.

Isobel turned her face into the rough warmth of the plaid and sobbed the long quivering sobs of utter desolation.

CHAPTER
THREE

A DENSE smoke filled the yard as they rode away on the ponies. They had heaped the heather stems of Isobel's marriage bed on the weed-grown cobbles and set light to them. Somehow she thought it was a grim symbol: of the past from which she had been so cruelly torn, of the dreams for the future which would never now rise from the ashes of this summer day. She was Hector Mac-Lean's wife, and there would be no escape as long as she lived.

The bitter tears of half an hour ago had given way to a numb misery which shut out any interest in her surroundings or the brightness of the day more surely than did the veiling smoke. She no longer cared what became of her, for the very worst had happened. She thought, without interest, that it was strange that they should be riding now in the same sunlit afternoon through which they had brought her here. Her life, which this morning had seemed so hopeful and full of the possibilities of happiness, lay now in ruins about her, and only an hour or two had passed. So short a time, and so complete a catastrophe.

She noticed, too, that the clergyman was no longer in sight: he had done his part, and gone quietly home again. Did he have any tremor of conscience at what he had done? Probably not, for her brief and painful acquaintance with Hector told her that he would have made very sure that no suspicion of the truth would trouble the minister. Without doubt he believed them to be a devoted couple, running away to new happiness together.

She became aware, after a while, that the men who surrounded her, on horse or on foot, were fewer than they had been at that dreadful moment in the wood. Hector was there still, of course, silent and preoccupied at her side, as if he had forgotten her existence; and there were four others, as far as she could see without glancing too obviously about her. But the three High-landers who had acted as witnesses to her marriage were nowhere to be seen, nor most of the men who had brought her here or awaited her arrival at the cottage. She wondered for a moment if Hector would tell her what had become of them, were she to ask. But when she stole a cautious glance in his direction his expression was so forbidding that she did not dare to intrude. Most likely he had felt that too large a company riding together might attract unwelcome attention.

Even less did she dare to ask where he was taking her. To his home, she supposed: to a place called Ardshee, if his name were any guide. But where that was she had no idea. She could only guess that it must lie somewhere to the north of the threatening range of mountains she had never thought to cross. Yet, when she looked about her, she realised that they were not going to cross them even now. They were not riding towards them at all, but parallel with them, in what she guessed to be a south westerly direction. The level plain grew more hilly, and the hills rose until they met the mountains, but still they did not turn north. Their only change of direction came when, now and then, they made a detour to avoid a town or village or farmhouse. But there was no comfort for Isobel in their unexpected route. The one certainty about it, wherever it took them, was that each mile bore her relentlessly further and further from all she knew and loved.

After a time weariness began to drive out even her misery. She thought of her soft bed at home, her quiet room, the gentle attentiveness of her parents. She began to think that if only Hector would allow them to pause now and rest she would not mind so much about all that had happened. And then she remembered that her bed would no longer be a place of rest and refuge for her, ever. She had a husband now, a husband in every sense

of the word, and she could never hope to shut herself off
from his demands. Despair swept her again, and tears
began to run slowly down her face.

If Hector noticed her unhappiness he showed no sign.
Their steady pace did not flag. It was early evening now,
and the sun was full in their faces, a fiery ball sliding
down towards the smooth flame-edged line of the horizon, stretching a broad path across . . . across . . .

Isobel was jerked in an instant out of her grief. It was
the sea which faced them, a few short miles away. The
sea dancing in the little evening breeze, sparkling beneath the rosy light of the setting sun. The sea on which a
little fleet of fishing boats bobbed black on the waves,
and further out a larger ship, sails furled, stood at
anchor.

Terror seized her. She knew now why they had not
crossed the mountains. Ardshee lay across the sea. They
would take her from the land of her birth to some bleak
island cut off by storms and wild weather for half the
year. It would be a banishment more terrible than
anything she could have imagined. Instinctively, she
gave a little cry, and saw almost at once that Hector's
hand had moved swiftly to his dirk.

'Any trouble, and I'll use it,' said his eyes, and she did
not doubt their message. The thought crossed her mind
fleetingly that if he were to murder her he would not see
a penny of her fortune. But she was not—yet—so desperate as that.

Obedient to his unspoken command she swallowed
her tears and the journey was resumed as if there had
been no interruption. But that tiny momentary outcry
seemed to have stirred some numbed place in her mind
to new life, for she was thinking fast.

From the moment when Hector possessed her in the
loft she had come to a dull acceptance of that fact, and its
implications: she was his wife for ever and ever, until
death at last came to release her. There was no way out.
But now, like a sudden gleam of sunlight through the
dreary fog of her despair, came a reviving doubt. Was
that really true? Was there really no escape? If she fled

now from Hector, surely the law must protect her? Nothing which had happened today had come upon her by her own choice. She had been terribly, deeply wronged: she had been kidnapped and raped, and that brief marriage ceremony could surely mean nothing set against those bleak facts. She had no illusions about her future, even without Hector. Soiled as she was now, no other man would ever want her—even gentle John Campbell, for he was the most correct, the most upright of men. But if somehow she could escape, if the law would free her . . . Oh, for peace and solitude, and the loving care of her parents! She could ask for nothing more.

Yet there, ahead of them, lay the sea, and on its shores, perhaps, a boat to take them to Ardshee. If once Hector had her on board she knew that her hope of escape would be lost.

She glanced round. Hector's expression was as preoccupied as ever, but she did not allow herself to be misled. That cat-like instinct of his would warn him of any false move on her part almost before she made it. Another man, on horseback at her other side, was very likely as prepared for any emergency as his chieftain. And the other two Highlanders who loped tirelessly behind and in front of her would not even be handicapped by the need to control a frightened mount in the event of trouble; in any case, one of them had a firm grasp on her pony's bridle.

Yet if there were other people about—onlookers, who might see her need and come to her aid . . . Would Hector dare to use that long-bladed dirk if there were impartial witnesses to seize him and swear to his crime in a court of law?

Ahead of them lay a little cluster of houses, neat and white, gathered on the shore. Isobel prayed that this time they would not pass them by.

They were close enough to see clearly the small figures of a woman and child in one of the gardens, gathering in the day's washing, when Hector gave the soft-voiced instruction to turn into a little wind-scarred wood at the road side. Isobel's heart sank. Was this the end of her final desperate hope?

They crossed the wood and emerged into a meadow on the other side. The wind had risen now, and blew fiercely off the sea into their sun-dazzled faces. Now—if only they were closer to some kind of help—now was the moment to risk an escape. But the houses were still some way off, and the fields were deserted. If she tried to break free from them they would retake her easily. As they rode she gazed longingly at the little settlement, now well to their right. On their present course they would reach the shore several hundred yards from the houses.

And then, just as the last grains of hope were sliding from her, they turned again, northwards, straight towards the village. A thin line of wind-blown trees shielded them from inquisitive eyes as they approached a low stone cottage set just a little apart from the others. Hector must have friends there, she thought. Yes, for on the narrow stretch of beach beside it a boat was drawn up, and a knot of people waited, dark against the low sun. A wall reached from the shore to the house, providing a screen from prying neighbours.

Isobel's eyes swept rapidly over the scene, seeking for anything which might offer her that final chance. A gateway—an open space from which they could be seen by someone who might, just possibly might, help . . .

She found it at last. A narrow rutted lane was just visible through a break in the trees as they came nearer. It must link the cottage to the other houses, to whatever passed for a village street, perhaps. It ran along the inland side of the cottage and bent sharply, close to the neighbouring house, before disappearing from view. It was just possible . . .

She tried not to turn her head that way, for she dared give no clue to Hector, but her eyes never left the lane as they rode steadily nearer. All her thoughts were on it, and the hope it offered.

'Please,' she prayed silently, 'please let me find a way!'

Ten yards to go, before they must follow a little path to the shore, and the waiting boat. Ten yards . . . nine . . . eight . . . and the man holding her pony stumbled briefly on a half-hidden stone in the path. Just for that moment his grasp was less than firm. Just long enough for Isobel to reach out and drag the halter into her hands, and dig her heels firmly into the pony's rough sides. He snorted, and shied, and leapt into a headlong gallop.

Isobel thrust her fingers into his mane and held on. She could not begin to guide him, at that frantic pace. She could only be thankful that he was carrying her inland, towards the gardens where they had seen the woman and child.

Behind her came shouts, and the thudding of hooves. She kicked the pony again. Better a broken neck, than to be back in Hector's hands . . .

Three women stood talking at a back door. She called out:

'Help me! Oh please help me!'

She saw the faces turned towards her, white, open-mouthed—and then the thudding hooves were upon her, passing her—a pony swung across her path, a hand reached out.

Her mount came to a shuddering halt, almost throwing her, and she looked up at the tall Highlander who faced her. She remembered him dimly from the ruined cottage—one of the witnesses to that mockery of a marriage. She gave a cry and threw herself from the pony's back, as fast as her legs could carry her, towards the women—

But he was too quick. His hand was on her arm, she struggled wildly—and a fierce blow sent her down into whirling darkness.

She came to rest at last, on a hard prickly surface. Her head throbbed fiercely, each cruel spasm passing through her so that it seemed as if her body was never still. She opened her eyes to darkness, but even that little effort hurt her, flooding her with a wave of nausea. She closed them again, and lay while the throbbing lessened slightly, and waited for the dizzy pounding to cease.

It was some time before she realised that the movement was not all in her head. The whole room was swaying, rocking from side to side with strange rhythmic creaks and the whining of wind. A deep throbbing sound, like the distant eerie chanting of ghostly voices, underlined each rise and fall. She opened her eyes again, and let them grow accustomed to the dark, and sent out exploring fingers at her sides.

She found that she lay in a small enclosed space, on a rough mattress on a hard wooden floor. All she could see, even now, was a faintly discernible square of lesser darkness, deeply blue and lit from time to time with stars: the night sky, passing from sight with each tilt of the room. She understood at last: she was on board a ship.

She sat up sharply, forgetting her head until a sickening clangour made her raise her hand to her eyes and groan aloud. It was only then that she discovered she was not alone. A dark figure emerged from somewhere below that dim square, and took shape, towering blackly over her. She heard him fumble around for a moment or two, then a sudden flame shot into the dark, steadied, and the glow of a lantern lit the cabin.

It was the face she had last seen before darkness closed in which looked into hers now. It was pale and grotesque in the lantern light, the strong bones white against the fiery shades of the hair. Instinctively she shrank back as he bent closer. But all he did was to scrutinise her carefully for a moment before placing the lantern on the floor and going to the door. He had to bend to go through it, she saw.

He shouted loudly in Gaelic, and she heard an answering call from somewhere outside. After a few moments Hector came, stooping scarcely at all as he passed the other man and came to stand at her side. The door closed softly, and they were alone. His eyes, dark like those of the man who had left them, yet had none of the malicious gleam she had faced just now.

But there was little to comfort her in that. For this was the man who had brought her here, and ruined her life. And if, as she thought, the red-haired Highlander had struck the blow which felled her in her moment of flight, it was for Hector he did it, and at Hector's command.

Helpless, she lay back on the hard mattress and gazed at him with listless unhappy eyes. His expression, watching her, was as enigmatic as ever, though she thought there was satisfaction in it somewhere.

'So, Mrs MacLean,' he said softly, 'you have come to your senses at last. You did a foolish thing. You might have been killed.'

She wondered fleetingly whether the runaway pony or the red-haired Highlander had posed the greater threat to her life, but there seemed little point in asking. She said only, in a voice harsh between dry lips:

'Or I might have escaped from you—'

He smiled faintly, and shook his head.

'No, Isobel, not that. Not ever.'

She shivered, and moved to turn her face away from him: but the effort needed was too much for her. She closed her eyes instead.

'They will bring food and drink,' Hector went on briskly. 'Then you will be better.'

She doubted it, but she found he was right, to some degree. The food was unexciting, but she was hungrier than she had expected, and the rough bread was fresh and satisfying, the cheese good, the water clear and cool. They left her alone while she ate, and when she had finished she fell into the deep sleep of exhaustion.

When she woke again a watery gleam of sunlight slanted across the floor of the tiny cabin. She noticed, too, that the fierce heaving of the boat had subsided to a gentle, barely perceptible, rocking motion. Had they reached their destination?

She sat up, relieved that her head no longer ached, though she could still feel the bruise on her skull. She could almost reach the door from her bed, so small was the room, but not quite. She rose cautiously onto unsteady legs and took the two steps which brought the latch within reach of her hand.

It was locked, of course. She might have known that it would be. She moved instead to the little square window, and felt the cool freshness of sea wind on her face: there was no glass in it. The grey-blue surface of the sea beyond dazzled her eyes after the dimness of her room. They must be close to the shore, for she could see a thin edge of green beyond the water, as of a hillside rising steeply. It was very quiet. There was no sound of feet on the deck, no clamour of voices, no land-noises from further off. Only the solitary mournful mewing cry of a gull broke the silence.

She stood gazing out and listening for some time, and then sudden panic seized her. Where were they all? What had happened? Was she alone here on the ship, locked up, in some deserted harbour where she would never be found?

She ran to the door and began to pound on it with her fists: the sound seemed pitifully feeble against the gentle lap of the waves, the cry of the gulls.

'Where are you? Let me out!' she cried, her voice breaking with disuse and terror. And then relief overwhelmed her as she heard an answering step from outside. Even the company of that grim follower of Hector's would be preferable to being deserted, a forgotten prisoner, on some strange coast. She sank down on the mattress and waited.

It was Hector himself who came in, his brows drawn together in a frown. 'What ails you, woman?' he demanded. 'You've all you need, have you not? There is no call for you to be making that din.'

'All I need!' she thought, gazing at him wide-eyed. 'How could anyone be so stupid, so insensitive? I am his prisoner, taken from all I know and love, and he can imagine for one moment that I have all I need!' A great lump threatened to choke her, and she felt the tears fill her eyes, but she would not let them fall. 'He shall not have that satisfaction,' she thought. Fiercely, she cleared her throat and asked, as coolly as she could:

'What has happened? Have we reached your . . . where . . .?'

'Ardshee?' He shook his head. 'We are anchored here until the wind changes, to give the rowers a rest. That is all.'

He was silent then, and stood looking down at her, deep in some unreadable thoughts of his own. She watched him uncomfortably, unable to think of anything to say, but longing to break the silence.

In the end he broke it himself, saying abruptly: 'They are on shore just now.'

So we are alone, she thought; not quite sure why that should make her shiver.

But a moment later she knew: for he reached out suddenly and drew her to her feet and into his arms, his grasp relentless about her. She struggled wildly, her palms against his shoulders, turning her head aside with close-shut mouth.

'No!' she cried. 'No!' 'Not again,' said her wildly thudding heart, and her weakening limbs, and she did not know what exactly it was that she feared.

Whatever it was there was no escape. His mouth found hers, warm, ruthless, demanding, and all her resistance melted, more quickly, more surely, than it had that first time. The protests of her brain were stilled, the words drowned in a wave of desire and longing. Her arms lifted and slid about his neck and he carried her to that narrow bed; and there, for the second time, Hector made her his own.

When, later, he had drawn away from her and straightened his clothes and left her without a word, she knew exactly what she had feared so much as his arms had closed about her. At that moment it had not been the harm he could do her which had frightened her, or the fact that she was a helpless captive, or her loneliness, or any other fear which would have been natural enough in the circumstances. No, what frightened her lay in herself, a terrible, newly-discovered weakness to which, shamefully, this man she hated held the key. One touch of his fingers, one fierce meeting of his mouth with hers,

and he had her entirely in his power, lost and helpless.
All her hatred, all she ought to feel for a man who had so
deeply wronged her, could be swept away in an instant
by the wild call of his blood to hers. Only for that little
while, until, his lust satisfied, he had turned from her, all
interest gone; only until the shame and self-disgust
swept over her, that she should be so weak.

Trembling now, she closed her eyes and clenched her
fists and tried somehow to believe that when next
he came to her—as he surely would—she could meet his
passion with coldness, and anger, and resistance. But
the lingering contentment of her body, half-naked on
the narrow bed, gave the lie to her hopes. Perhaps, in
time, when passion was no longer new to her, or
strange . . .

Voices calling on deck roused her from her thoughts,
and a little later they brought more food to her. And
then, towards evening, the creaking of timbers, the
resumption of the strange chanting song of the oarsmen,
the rapidly increasing motion of the boat, told her that
they had set sail once more. She did not see Hector again
that day.

CHAPTER
FOUR

THE night seemed interminable. Isobel could not sleep
again, for last night's rest had taken the edge from her
exhaustion and she was too unhappy to be able to find
that refuge from her misery. Even to lie on the bed,
inactive, became too much of an ordeal, for then the
confused, bewildering emotions, the dreadful fears, rose
up clamorously in her brain and brought her close to
crying out.

So for most of the night she paced the uneven floor of
the tiny cabin, or stood at the window, gazing out at the
black heaving waters, finding a little refreshment in the
salt spray on her face.

Once she wept, long slow sobs which went on and on
as if her heart would break. But in the end that too
ceased to offer any relief, for she had no hope of
comfort.

At home, or during the years of James Carnegie's
illness, even at her worst moments there had always
been friends to bring her affection and tenderness,
people who loved her and wanted to help her. It had
never been as bad as this.

That, she thought, was the worst part of her present
plight. To be so alone, amongst people who for the most
part could not even speak her language, who wanted her
money or her body, but cared nothing for the frightened
girl inside. Who seemed at times almost to hate her, if
the light in the eyes of the tall Highlander was any guide.
She did not know what kind of life she would have to
lead at her journey's end, but her instinct told her it
would be frighteningly alien to anything she knew. This
little ship, bobbing on the black waves, was carrying her
further and further into the unknown.

With relief she saw the dawn light creep into the sky. Nothing would seem quite so bad in daylight as it had in the grim moments before dawn. But it did not help a great deal. She felt numb now, as if everything she did, all that happened to her, was part of a dream, grey and unreal. She had almost come to believe that soon she would wake, and find herself in her own dear room at home with the birds chorusing joyously in the garden beyond the window—when the cabin door was flung wide and two Highlanders came and led her, one grasping each arm, into the daylight.

The shock of icy spray and sea wind flung in her face as she stepped onto the deck drove out any lingering doubt as to whether or not she was awake. But the scene before her stopped her in her tracks: nothing had prepared her for this.

The waves stretched silver grey and dancing to a mountainous shore, the dark rugged peaks outlined against a morning sky streaked with palest green and amethyst and rose. And as she watched the sun slid with copper brilliance over the horizon and the landscape woke to life.

Thick woods covered the nearer slopes, blue-shadowed and gold-edged like the mountain peaks above—kindly mountains, softened by young bracken and the gentler line of the trees. Here and there a burn splashed white into the sea, and higher up the silver gleam of a waterfall shone through the branches. To their left—towards the west—a small loch broke into the shoreline, blue and calm under the morning sky, and straight ahead a solitary, single-towered castle perched arrogantly upon a rocky headland, the waves tossing their spray upon the rocks at its feet.

A soft exclamation broke into her wondering trance, and Isobel turned her head to see Hector near to her, gazing as intently as she had done at the shore. She saw, with astonishment, that his dark eyes were bright with tears. She knew, then, where they were.

He noticed her at last and came, laughing, and flung his arm about her waist, crying out joyously in his own language. His delight touched her briefly, and she longed to understand him, but one glance at the hesitation in her eyes drove from him all trace of that moment of warmth. He drew away, and turned to the tall Highlander at his other side, and they were lost in excited talk, forgetting her.

The wonder of the sunrise had evaporated now, unrecoverable. The rowers, who had paused for a moment in acknowledgement of its splendour, bent again to their work, their voices raised more vigorously than ever in the rhythmic chanting song which lightened their task. Isobel stared at the swiftly-approaching land, and tried to find some clue as to what awaited her.

Ardshee: that, she supposed, must be the name of the castle and its land, for they were turning slightly east beneath it and making for a little bay, half hidden by the rocky headland. As they entered it, passing the castle on their left, the wind dropped suddenly, the waves were still, the chanting ceased, and a great quietness fell over the ship.

Around the bay, sheltering it, towered great rock-strewn cliffs, softened by trees which grew even where the slope seemed almost vertical: oak, rowan, birch, clinging against all the odds to rock and grass, vibrantly golden-green in the early light, though the sun still scarcely reached the mouth of the bay. As the ship moved into the shadow the echoing chorus of a thousand bird voices reached them, as if struck up in welcome.

A cry from the land disturbed the tranquillity, and Isobel's gaze moved to the narrow shingle beach which fringed the bay at the foot of the trees. There, where the shoreline widened out in the innermost corner of the bay, half a dozen or so thatched stone huts huddled as if for shelter. And from them men were running, gathering on the beach with an accompaniment of excited shouting which echoed against the cliff walls.

Close to the shore the ship grounded gently, its single square sail furled, its oars drawn into the side, the rowers scrambling to their feet and stretching cramped limbs. Isobel wondered how they were to reach the land, for there were still several yards of cold dancing water between ship and shore.

And then, astonishingly, there was a sudden dramatic pause. She saw the rowers turn their heads towards the prow, saw Hector step forward to the side of the ship, the tall Highlander a pace or two behind him. And then a small stately clansman took up his position close to his chieftain, hoisted bagpipes to his mouth, and began to play.

Isobel had not often heard the bagpipes played, and had the lowest opinion of their musical qualities; but she had to admit to herself, now, that this was different. A solemn melody, full of grandeur, following a strange intricate informal pattern of its own, carried over the quiet water. It was like some old tale, full of heroic phrases and magnificent language, weaving a fabric of brave deeds and noble sacrifice. It was not music as she knew it, but it had unexpected power, and somehow it was entirely suited to the wild landscape and the appearance of the listeners, grave-faced, barbaric, yet suddenly dignified.

She glanced at Hector, a motionless figure but for the quiver of the eagle's feather in his blue bonnet and the fluttering of his plaid. His eyes were bright, with pride and some warmer emotion, and his expression had something of the solemnity appropriate to a man taking part in a religious ceremony.

Then, all at once, the pipes leapt into a lively martial rhythm, and the spell was broken. There was a splash, and Isobel saw that one of the men had already jumped into the water and was running towards the shore, heedless of the waves beating about his bare legs. Laughing, shouting, the rest followed, greeting their friends on the beach with handclasps and embraces. Two men stood knee-deep in the sea and reached up to lift Hector and carry him shoulder-high to dry land, cheered on by the others, and the piper strode through the water at their side to serenade his return.

Just as Isobel had begun to fear herself forgotten, the tall Highlander guided her to the side of the ship, swung himself into the water, and lifted her over into his arms. As easily—and carelessly—as if she were merely a sack of hay he carried her to the shore and set her down on the beach. And then, his duty done, he rejoined his chieftain, now almost hidden in a clamouring throng of delighted clansmen.

Isobel's legs felt strange, unsteady, as if they needed the rocking of the boat to give them strength. She stood alone where the small waves lapped the shingle and looked about her, shivering a little with fear and loneliness rather than with cold.

Here, close to the clustering huts, any charm they might have from a distance disappeared. They were roughly built, she could see that, of large rounded stones without mortar, the weather-beaten heather thatch giving them a ragged appearance. And over them all hung an unpleasant smell: the stink of dirt, and damp, and poverty, of animals and humans living too close for comfort or cleanliness.

Not, she reflected, that there were any animals to be seen, beyond a lean dog scavenging among the scraps on the midden nearby, and two scrawny hens. Nor even many humans, she realised, looking about her. Three men only were left on the shore, calling to a fourth still busy on the ship. The piper and most of the others had set out with Hector and the tall Highlander along a little path which curved its way up the slope from the bay, and then turned along the headland towards the castle. The huts had a look of desolate decay, as if they had been long deserted. Yet the men who had run to meet them had come from them.

Isobel shivered again, her dislike of the little settlement growing with every moment. She drew her cloak closer about her and turned to follow Hector and his companions.

The path twisted narrowly through thickly growing trees, rising sharply at first, and then levelling out at the summit of the headland to turn back on itself and follow the cliff edge, still sheltered by trees but offering dizzy glimpses of the deep wrinkled blue of the water hun-

dreds of feet below. Then, all at once, the path left the
wood, and emerged into the sunlight, dazzlingly bright,
striking a glittering shimmer from the surface of the sea,
forcing her to shade her eyes momentarily against its
glare.

Here, the headland narrowed sharply, its rocky surface spread with rough grasses, heather, bracken and
bog myrtle to the point where the castle stood, a single
solid rectangle of red-grey stone, sharply outlined on its
little hill against the cloudless sky.

She knew, in some part of her brain, that this was
Hector's home, now hers. But the knowledge was unreal, and meant nothing to her. From the moment of
landing everything had been so strange, so alien, that
she could not really believe she had any part in it. The
very air was unfamiliar, warm and soft and languorous,
heavy with the fragrance of bog myrtle and spiced with
the tang of the sea.

The fact that everyone ignored her only added to the
oddness of the sensation, as if she were a disembodied
observer from another world, a world which seemed
thousands of miles—centuries even—away from here.
Hector had been her one tenuous link with the familiar
and the loved, for once he had stood beneath the
orchard trees, but now even he was out of sight, beyond
a rocky outcrop that edged the path. A dream would
have seemed more real, for so often then the sleeper
knew that wakefulness, and the familiar everyday world,
were one short breath away, beyond the closed lids.
From this, for Isobel, there was no waking.

As she reached the rocks which had hidden Hector
from view, Isobel saw him again, not quite so far ahead,
where the path became a tiny track rising steeply to the
heavy studded door within its primitive arch, which
formed the only entrance of the castle. As they
approached, one of the party gave a shout and the door
opened. Yet another Highlander stood there, the piper
struck up another joyful but martial tune, and two
deerhounds, as lean and alert as Hector himself, leapt
out to greet him in a frenzy of barking and waving tails. It

was then, just as he reached out to fondle the hounds, that Hector remembered he had a wife: which was, presumably, the sole reason for his absence from home. He turned, and saw her, and said something to his companion. And with a sinking heart Isobel watched the tall man come towards her.

He did not relish the errand, she could see that. Very likely he would much rather have shared the homecoming of his master, joined in the laughter, walked in with them to the fire and refreshment made ready in the draughty hall inside the door. Instead, his expression was surly as he led Isobel indoors, to a door which opened from the hall to a winding stone stair.

Silently, obediently, she climbed the stair before him, round and round until they reached a small landing. Here, he opened another door, ushering her through. She heard the door close behind her and saw that she was alone.

It was a large room, not very much smaller than the hall below. And it surprised her. It was unmistakably the great bedchamber of an ancient castle, its narrow windows set deep in the thickness of the wall, the door heavily studded, the furnishings made with all the solid simplicity of another age. Yet it was not the primitive place she had expected.

The hangings on the carved oak bed were old and worn, the boards of the floor darkened with age, but an oriental carpet lay over them, much trodden though it was, and the walls were panelled. There were books arranged on a shelf in one corner, and a modern table set against one wall with a mirror standing on it, and a padded stool before it.

She went over to the table and examined the objects laid on its polished surface: an inlaid hair brush, a matching comb, and a small carved box containing a silver brooch of intricate Celtic design. They were fine articles, such as a lady of wealth and fashion might be glad to own, not what she would have expected to find in the room of a barbaric tribal chieftain. If it was his room.

A single picture hung on the wall near the table, a

portrait of a woman in a white gown crossed by a tartan scarf. Her dark eyes, the springing dark hair which framed her oval face, were somehow disconcertingly familiar. Isobel did not like to linger long under the gaze of those painted eyes.

She moved on to examine the bookshelves, and studied the leather covers, well-worn from use. A Latin grammar, a Bible, a number of works in Latin and French and English which any reasonably well-educated man might be expected to have on his shelves, some poetry. All a little old-fashioned, and very much like the selection James Carnegie kept in his library. Except that his books were rarely used. They were not, she thought, a lady's books. But she was not sure what they told her about this room, or its owner.

She took down the Latin grammar and opened it. Inside the cover the name 'Hector MacLean' was inscribed, in a careful schoolboyish writing. So they were his. But they did not fit at all with what she knew of the wild young man who had kidnapped her and brought her here and was even now drinking in the hall with his men and listening to the uncouth music which reached her faintly from below.

A chest, carved like the bed, stood at its foot. She went to it and lifted the lid. Inside lay a plaid, neatly folded, a few well-laundered shirts, a tooled leather belt decorated with loops of silver, and, unaccountably, a coat of rich wine-coloured brocade. It was a little old-fashioned in cut, but would not have looked out of place in her parents' best parlour. She found it impossible to imagine Hector dressed in anything so civilised. More in keeping was the sword which lay beside it, running the whole length of the chest. It was a massive weapon, broad-bladed and basket-hilted, and surely far too heavy for any but a giant to lift. She ran her finger over the entwined pattern which decorated the blade, deep in thought, and then slowly replaced the garments she had disturbed and closed the lid.

There was little else in the room to tell her anything about its usual occupant, if such he were. Only a high-backed arm chair, and a door which opened to reveal a cupboard in the thickness of the wall, containing a pair of shiny buckled shoes, an odd heavy round object with a vicious central spike which looked like some kind of primitive war shield, and not much else. A simple table at the bedside completed the furnishings. A tidy well-cared-for room, not luxurious, but clean and neat and almost comfortable: it did not fit at all.

And then Isobel realised what was most strange about this place, about their arrival, and the decaying settlement, and the castle. What, above all, had made it seem so unreal. There were no women.

There were men of all ages—bent and white-haired, middle aged, scarcely bearded. And they had homes, of sorts; and someone must care for this room, with its polished dust-free surfaces and spotless floor; and someone must have set the glasses ready downstairs at the fireside. But there were no women to be seen; no women and no children. Except for the woman in the portrait, and Isobel MacLean, wife to a man who grew stranger, more unknown with every second which passed.

She went to one of the windows and sat on the wide sill, padded with a cushion of faded blue velvet, and looked out over the sea. Only it was not the sea on which her eyes first rested. She gave a little exclamation and pressed her face close to the small leaded panes of the window.

Strange that she should not have noticed before, but on the ship her eyes had been turned to the shore where she must land, and, later, on her way along the path, she had been concerned only with the castle. Now she saw that the headland on which the castle stood reached out towards another shore. Two miles, perhaps, separated Ardshee from the more mountainous land across the sea, where dark purple-blue slopes rose from shore to sky. Another island, she supposed. She had not seen a map of her homeland, but she knew that the wild western Highlands were bordered with innumerable islands, of all shapes and sizes, like pieces roughly broken from the untamed mainland and scattered in the

unpredictable sea. She had guessed, of course, that
Ardshee lay on one of these, cut off more firmly than
ever from the decencies of civilisation. She had not
expected that another would lie quite so near.

Or was it, perhaps, not an island at all? Could it be the
mainland at which she gazed now? Wild, mountainous,
full of dangers, but the same land mass on which her
parents lived their ordered lives, and John Campbell
walked in the sunlit garden.

She felt a little shiver of excitement, which was not
quite hope. And then, behind her, the door opened, and
closed, and Hector came in.

He stood there saying nothing for a moment. There
was an air of good humour about him which had, she
knew, nothing to do with her. Though he did not smile.

'Did they bring you water to wash?' he asked after a
while.

She shook her head. 'No,' she said, standing up.

He went to the door and opened it and spoke to
someone just outside. She heard steps hurrying away
down the stairs before the door closed again.

'They will bring food too,' he said. And then he
crossed to the chest and drew out the plaid she had seen.
'When you have washed,' he went on, 'you may put this
on.' He held it out to her, but she made no move to take
it. She wrinkled her nose with distaste.

'That?' she exclaimed. 'What do you take me for?'

All trace of good humour left him at her words.

'May I tell you, madam,' he said harshly, 'that I think
you deeply unworthy ever to wear the plaid. You, a
Lowlander—an enemy of my race—!' The final pause
was more eloquent than any words.

Isobel gazed at him wide-eyed, shocked by the hate—
worse, by the contempt—in his tone and in his eyes. He
had said the word 'Lowlander' as her mother would have
said 'Highlander', with loathing and detestation. It gave
her an odd sensation, chilling and repelling her.

'Why . . .?' she began. She found that she could
scarcely speak. 'Why then . . .?'

'Why do I ask you to wear the plaid?' he finished for

her. 'Because you are, nevertheless, my wife—and have you seen how you look?'

She went to the mirror then, and studied herself. She had to admit that the last two days had left their mark upon her. Not only was she dirty and dishevelled, but her gown was torn and muddy, her cloak stained with salt water. Even a plaid might be better than that—at least in Hector's eyes.

She turned to him again.

'If I am so much beneath your contempt,' she asked in a low voice, ' why then did you marry me?' But even as she spoke she knew it was a foolish question, for she knew the answer and it could only hurt her more to hear him confirm it.

He laughed faintly, with derision.

'For your money, of course,' he said. 'What did you think?'

She turned away, sick at heart, and wandered to the window.

'What possible use can my money be to you here?' she asked wearily. 'There's nothing to buy, and nothing to spend it on.'

'There speaks all the comfortable ignorance of the wealthy,' he mocked her. 'Did you not see how my people are living? Can you not guess that they want sound roofs and good clothes and a doctor? And a school perhaps, and help to grow better crops and to keep their animals from sickness.'

She gazed at him in astonishment.

'You wanted my money for that!'

'Is that so strange?' he returned.

She could think of no reply, except that Hector was still an enigma to her. And then she remembered her thoughts of a few moments ago.

'But why do you need schools? I have seen no children—and why are there no women?'

He smiled then, briefly, almost with pity.

'I forget you know nothing of our way of life. They are at the shieling, the women and children together, with the animals. They will stay there until the autumn, while the men repair the houses before the storms, and the cattle grow fat on good grass. When you have eaten we shall ride there, so the women and children may see my bride.'

'And are you not ashamed to show them a Lowlander?' she asked sharply.

'Ah, but they know what you bring with you,' he said.

'But I haven't brought it with me—and you may never lay your hands on it,' she retorted, with a little gleam of triumph.

'You are my wife,' he said simply, as though no other reply were necessary. And then he turned away to admit the man who brought warm water in a silver bowl, and a tray set with food and drink. 'Make yourself ready quickly,' he said. 'I will return for you shortly.'

Washing and eating presented no problem, though Isobel shivered in the chill of the room as she stripped off the soiled garments. There was no fire in the wide hearth, and the solid walls admitted little warmth from the summer day.

Once she had eaten and washed, however, and replaced her petticoat, Isobel gazed at the plaid in perplexity. Where, she thought, does one begin with this vast expanse of cloth? She tried to wind it about her, first this way and then that, becoming only progressively more entangled, and more dismayed. Hector had thought her unworthy even to wear this garment. What would he say if he knew she had no idea how to put it on?

She was close to tears by the time he returned. He smiled derisively.

'Yes,' he said, 'I see you are very much the Lowlander. The plaid has defeated you.'

But he came to her side and took the length of material and deftly draped it about her, securing it at the waist with the belt from the chest, and at the breast with the circular silver brooch from the little box.

'There,' he commented. 'Now you are more fitting to appear as my bride.'

She fingered the brooch, trying to accustom herself to the strange feel of the plaid about her. She had to admit that Hector had constructed a most effective garment from it.

'It was my mother's,' he added, and it took her a moment or two to realise that he referred to the brooch.

'Oh . . .' she said, and then she indicated the brush and comb. 'Were all those hers, then?'

'Indeed they were—and there is her likeness.' His hand swept towards the portrait. The dark eyes, so like his own, gazed shrewdly at the tall graceful figure of his wife, as if they recognised the fear and misery tightening into a knot behind the silver brooch.

As Hector took her arm, and they turned to leave the room, Isobel caught a glimpse of herself in the mirror, and for a moment was startled. She had grown so used to her image clothed in matronly grey, or mourning black. Now, with the plaid draped in soft folds about her shoulders and her head, she looked unlike herself, the bright yet subtle colours of the tartan drawing colour even from her weary face. And she looked, too, as primitive as the Highlanders around her: another person, no longer the Isobel Carnegie who had left the kirk two mornings ago. It was an uncomfortable sensation, as if she had glimpsed a stranger.

As she followed Hector from the room she wondered whether the person inside the enveloping plaid still had anything in common with the young widow of so short a time before.

CHAPTER
FIVE

THEY rode sturdy ponies to the shieling. The piper went with them, and the inevitable tall Highlander. Isobel was fast growing to hate his presence as Hector's constant shadow. The other clansmen followed them on foot, and the deerhounds ran alongside, veering off at intervals in pursuit of elusive scents.

They took a steep winding track to the mountainside above the cliffs, where the rocky landscape was spread with grass and bracken and wild flowers. Little knots of stunted birch and hazel and rowan grew in the sheltered hollows, and bog-myrtle scented the air. A breeze blew off the sea, but gently, just enough to take any discomfort from the heat of the mid-morning sun.

They had gone perhaps two miles when they saw a small black figure outlined against the sky, like a sentinel keeping watch from the rising ground. Either it was further away than it seemed, Isobel thought, or it was a child; and even as she narrowed her eyes to see better he disappeared. A few moments later a crowd of dark figures appeared in his place, large and small, waving, calling out, their excitement visible even at this distance.

The approaching riders were almost swallowed up in the eager group as they reached the hill top. Hands reached out, voices were raised in lilting greeting, tousle-haired children jumped up and down. The welcome was for Hector, and he returned it warmly, dismounting to continue the short journey to the shieling on foot, asking questions of this one and that—Isobel could not understand what he said, but she could guess at the enquiries about the health of one and the child of another from the expressions and gestures of the women as Hector addressed them.

To Isobel they were cool, but respectful and courteous. And she sensed beneath the rather distant words
and gestures an immense curiosity about her. Good
manners kept it in check, but she glimpsed covert
glances stolen in her direction, remarks exchanged in an
undertone when they thought she was not looking. She
could see that they thought her beautiful, and were
surprised at it, but she knew they were judging her too.
They were making guesses at the quality of this foreign
bride of their chieftain, the woman who was to bring
them riches and hope for a better future. She sat stiffly
on the ambling pony, and tried to gaze ahead at nothing
in particular so that she should not see the speculative
eyes turned on her.

Beyond the rise the land dipped into a wide hollow.
Sheltered on the windward side by tall pines, watered by
a little burn, it lay bathed in sunlight, a natural haven on
the bleak mountainside. Here a rough circle of simple
turf huts, like large beehives, had been constructed,
grouped in pairs, and close by shaggy cattle grazed on
the soft hill grass.

In one place a cooking pot bubbled on a fire burning in
a raised stone hearth, in another dishes of cream lay
ready for making cheese or butter, with the wooden
butter churns beside them. Washing was spread on the
grass to dry. And as the welcoming women led Hector
and the menfolk into the hollow the sound of singing
filled it, and the whole place seemed alight with happiness.

Once again Isobel had that overwhelming sense of
unreality. She understood nothing that was said, no
words of the songs, little of this foreign way of life. She
was left at the end of that day with no more than a
confused impression of the simple but joyous feasting
which welcomed the Chieftain and his bride.

When Hector had helped her from her pony he led her
to a quiet place beside one of the huts where an old
woman sat on a stool mending a plaid. She looked up as
they came near, her face glowing, her very blue eyes
bright with tears. She laid down her sewing and reached

out gnarled hands. And to Isobel's amazement Hector fell on his knees beside her and bent his head and the old woman leaned over to kiss his dark hair, murmuring soft endearments as he grasped her hand in both of his.

After a time he sat back on his heels and looked up at Isobel, while the old woman continued to run one hand caressingly over his hair.

'Isobel, I must make you known to my foster mother, Mairi MacLean.'

He turned to the old woman and said something in his own language, and then took Isobel's hand and laid it in that of the other woman. Instinctively she knelt too, and she felt the hand laid on her head and the murmured words of blessing. When she looked up the old woman cupped her face in the work-worn hands and gazed into it long and silently, reading what lay there. Isobel felt as if her whole soul were laid bare. It frightened her, and she shivered a little; and yet she sensed kindness and understanding, as if she could find a friend there if she chose. But what use was a friend who could not even speak to her in her own language?

The greetings and introductions over, Hector lingered there to talk for a little longer and then led Isobel to where a rough seat had been prepared for her to one side of the hollow. The whole experience left her feeling an unaccustomed warmth towards her husband, now he had so openly exposed his emotions to her, and asked her to share a little of them. For the first time she almost liked him.

'Did your mother die when you were young?' she asked, as they crossed the trodden turf between the huts.

'Indeed no,' he replied, a little surprised. 'She died last year, soon after my father. I think they could not live long apart.'

'I thought that must be why you had a foster mother,' she explained.

The warmth began to fade as she saw that derisive smile pass briefly across his face. Clearly she had only succeeded in reminding him once more that she was a Lowlander, ignorant of Highland ways.

'It is the custom,' he told her. 'The son of the chieftain is always fostered until he reaches twelve years or so with a woman of the clan. Thus he grows at one with his people, and her children are his brothers.' He glanced across at the tall Highlander, who stood talking to a pretty black-haired girl. 'Hugh there is the son of Mairi MacLean and Seumas her man, now dead.'

Isobel's sense of isolation returned to her, and the last remnants of that incipient liking for Hector vanished without trace. In silence she allowed herself to be deposited on her solitary throne and abandoned to her painful reflections. A slow lilting song aching with grief and loss reached her, sung in a deep contralto voice, entirely in keeping with her thoughts.

They returned to Ardshee late in the day, seen on their way by the same group who had gathered on the hilltop this morning, the evening sun now full in their faces.

Isobel felt utterly weary now, and thought longingly of sleep. Even the recollection that Hector would lie beside her—she supposed—could not quell the longing.

But she found as they entered the castle that the coming of night did not mean that activity was at an end. In the hall, watched by a solemn portrait of Hector's father, as fair as his son was dark, a great fire was brought to life and the celebrating began in earnest.

Mutton was roasted, wine and whisky passed lavishly from hand to hand, the piper played ever more wildly. And there was no escape for Isobel. Hector led her to a carved oak chair near the hearth and there she sat, hour after hour, as the leaping flames lit the scene and the noise and movement set her head aching.

She had never before been the lone woman at the feasting of men. She knew that drink and the absence of the civilising company of women turned men to brute beasts, uncouth, full of lewd talk and unbelievable brutality. The thought of what she might have to face tonight filled her with fear.

And then they began to dance. Astonished, she forgot her weariness and watched wide-eyed. This was nothing

like the stately minuets she knew at home, nor the
light-hearted measures of the country people of the
Lowlands; but fierce warlike dancing, performed with
arrogance and grace and amazing skill.

She watched Hector dance alone, his slender feet in
their supple shoes moving with incredible lightness and
agility between the shining crossed blades of two great
swords, his plaid swinging, his eyes bright in his flushed
face. Head high, arms raised, his lithe body held as
proudly as if those busy feet were not a part of him, he
was like no man she had ever seen in her life before.
And in spite of herself a little of his excitement, and a
quiver of pride in his animal beauty reached her as she
watched.

Then all the clansmen were on the floor, and the noise
of the pipes became deafening. The figures dipped and
weaved and leapt, tartans swinging, the brilliant colours
blurring into a bewildering mass. Yet even now there
was a pattern. This was not an uncontrolled mob of men
sent wild by drink, but recognisably a dance in which each
knew his part and performed it neatly, so that the steps
followed from one to the other in orderly sequence.
And it seemed that the more they drank, the more
intricate the dancing became. For one fleeting moment
Isobel tried to imagine her father taking his part on the
floor before her, and she almost laughed aloud. It only
confirmed her feeling that these Highlanders were not
like other men. And that was a frightening thought, for
she knew how to deal with other men, how to appeal to
their tenderness, or win their sympathy.

She had no idea how long she sat there watching the
dancing. Perhaps now and then she dozed off: she was
not sure, for she lost all sense of time, and one dance
blurred into another. Her body ached for rest, but she
could not have struggled to her feet had she wanted to,
though the chair was hard and unyielding.

She had briefly drifted into sleep when a hand on her
shoulder shook her awake, and she opened her eyes to
find Hector, clearly very drunk by now, reaching down
to sweep her into his arms. Just as he had, she thought

dimly, in the cottage where he had married her. But she was too weary to struggle.

'Bed, my wife!' he cried, and she heard the encouraging shouts of his clansmen.

He carried her roughly up the winding stair through a darkness lit only dimly by a flickering torch carried some way behind. Once she glimpsed Hugh's gaunt face, lurid in the pale torch-light, as he followed them to light their way.

Then they were alone, and the longed-for bed was soft beneath her in the sudden total darkness. Sleep sucked her down, and she yielded to it, infinitely grateful for its relentless hold upon her. Somewhere, half-consciously, she was aware of Hector's hands tugging at the plaid he had wound about her, pulling off her petticoat, finding their way between her relaxed thighs. But this time there was no response from her weary body, no eager coming alive, no interest at all. She neither accepted nor resisted his eager possession of her, but was simply thankful when it ended and sleep claimed her completely.

One tiny thought only flickered through her weary brain before she fell asleep. That this time his love-making meant nothing to her, that it was something which happened without her will or her involvement. His one hold over her emotions had gone. She was smiling a little as she slid into unconsciousness.

A finger of sunlight touched Isobel's lids and woke her to the new day. She lay for a little while with her eyes closed, savouring the softness of pillow and feather mattress, the smoothness of clean linen sheets, the enclosing warmth of the bedclothes.

Another day. James was dead, her duty done. The future held hope for her. Today, as yesterday, there would be no call on her to do this or that. She was free. Free to sit in the parlour and read, to talk to her parents of this and that, to spend an hour or two in the still room or the garden. The sun was shining, and John Campbell might call, and they could ride or walk together. Life was good.

She turned onto her back, and smiled and stretched, enjoying the sunlight rosy on her closed lids.

And then she remembered.

With a shudder she rolled onto her side, knees drawn up, hands over her face. She felt cold now, and fear lurched in the pit of her stomach. She longed to return to the blissful unconsciousness of a moment ago. But there was no escape.

She opened her eyes, and there, watching her gravely, was Hector. Dark eyes, long-lashed, unfathomable as a mountain tarn. His dark hair hung loose about his face, touched with gleaming shades of bronze and chestnut in the sunlight. One long-fingered brown hand reached out towards her.

With a cry she retreated across the bed and onto the floor, cold to her bare feet. She gathered up the plaid from where it had fallen last night and pulled it about her, and then stood shivering, unable to think, as if mesmerised by his impenetrable gaze, aware only of terror and hopelessness.

He swore pungently in Gaelic and threw back the covers. He too was naked, bronzed and slender and muscular, perfectly proportioned. She watched him with a reluctant fascination as he crossed the room and flung his plaid about him, neatly kilting it about his waist before throwing the end over his shoulder. And then he went out, slamming the door behind him.

Isobel breathed deeply, from relief, and relaxed a little. But despair still hung heavy upon her. That moment of forgetfulness on first waking had been so real. It had only brought home to her the horror of her plight, and her loneliness.

She moved listlessly to the stool by the little table, but one glimpse of her own face in the mirror—the shadowed, frightened eyes looking back at her—was more than she could stand. She retreated to the window seat, and sat with her legs drawn up, huddled in the plaid.

The rosy morning sun was tinting the mountains across the sea. They were transformed, inviting. Was that indeed the mainland? If she could find and steal a boat, and cross that quiet stretch of water, would she then, somehow, be able to make her way home? But even as she wondered she knew it was hopeless.

They had made a two-day sea journey to reach here: very likely what she saw was just another island. And even if it were not, and she were to find her way there, she had no certainty of escape. Rather the reverse, for she knew nothing of boats, and Hector clearly knew a great deal, and it was most unlikely that she could hope to get far. And she had no idea at all which way to take once she reached those mountains. She would, almost certainly, die of exposure or starvation within days.

She was distracted from her gloomy thoughts by a movement close at hand below the window. Hector was there, talking animatedly to the inevitable Hugh and another man. His ill-humour seemed to have evaporated, for he was laughing. The dogs cavorted around him, clearly expecting an expedition of some kind. And after a moment the two foster-brothers parted from the other man and set off together inland, out of sight. Hunting, perhaps, thought Isobel, or to the shieling, or on some other mundane but unknown business. She was not really interested, but the knowledge that Hector had left her here, alone, where no one spoke her language, hurt her, though she had no reason to expect consideration from him. If only he had let her know what she should do with her day.

But she knew that he would not let her know because he did not care. She was inescapably his prisoner, and that was all that interested him. He must suppose that one day, before too long, he would also have her fortune in his hands. And apart from that she did not matter at all. 'I am not a person,' she thought bitterly. 'I am a Lowlander—a necessary evil, a way to bring prosperity to the clan. He does not think that I might have feelings. Very likely he thinks only Highlanders have feelings.'

She sat for a long time at the window until she grew numb with cold. Then she began slowly, shivering, to dress. She put on her petticoat, and then tried to remember how Hector had wound the plaid about her. It was not easy, and it took her a long time, but eventually she managed to contrive some kind of garment, held with brooch and belt. She had just finished when a man came to bring her food and drink.

He deposited bowl and spoon and cup in silence on the table and left her, with a faintly respectful gesture which was not quite a bow. Clearly Hector's men shared their chieftain's view of her.

The bowl contained porridge, which Isobel did not much like, though at least it was hot and filling, and there was milk in the cup. Afterwards, she felt her courage return a little, and wandered about the room in search of occupation. She stood before the books, scanning the titles in search of something absorbing enough to hold her attention despite her unhappiness. But neither a Latin Grammar nor Dryden's poetry seemed likely to offer such solace, and she knew no French. She walked restlessly back to the window.

And then, on impulse, she decided to explore the castle. She set out cautiously down the winding stair, pausing at every sound as if she feared discovery. In the hall two men stood talking at the fireside, but fell silent as soon as they saw her. Their eyes gazed back at her, unremittingly hostile.

Through the open main door of the castle the sunlight slanted, luring her beyond the reach of those unfriendly eyes. Swiftly she turned that way, and stepped out onto the grass. In the warm and fragrant air she felt just a little less burdened by her unhappiness. She stood looking about her for a moment, at the track which led to the bay, and then towards the rocks of the headland. She took that path in the end, clambering her way towards the black rocks against which the waves splashed. The water was deep, dark blue-green, patterned with sea-weed. And dangerous, she was sure of that.

She wandered on to a little shingly beach, and sat on a rock, throwing pebbles idly into the water. The tranquillity of the scene seeped gently into her, numbing her into some kind of unthinking trance. She forgot what had brought her here, all that had happened, almost who she was. The lap and swish of the waves, the plop of the pebbles into the water, filled her mind.

But it did not last. She had not seen the dark clouds massing in the west, streaming across the sky towards Ardshee. But a sudden cold scattering of rain woke her to reality. By the time she reached the castle sea and mountain were obliterated in a relentless curtain of grey.

She ran shivering to the bedroom and began to unwind the wet plaid. And then remembered she had nothing else to wear, and hesitated. Her soiled gown had been taken away for washing, and the cloak with it. She opened the chest and searched among the garments there, taking out a shirt and considering the brocade coat for a moment. In the end she rejected the coat and dressed in the shirt. It was of fine linen, frilled at neck and wrists, and not very warm. But at least it was dry. She laid the sodden plaid and petticoat over the stool, wishing for a fire, and then wrapped a blanket from the bed about her.

The rain beat unceasingly against the windows for the entire afternoon. Isobel slept a little, curled up in the bed, and tried, without success, to find something to interest her among Hector's books. Otherwise she sat or lay listening to the rain and wishing almost for Hector's company, as better than none.

He came home at last late in the day, drenched and good-humoured, and called at once for a fire to be lit. Isobel wondered if he had seen her sitting on the bed, for he said nothing to her as he came in.

'You did not have a fire lit for me,' she complained once the flames were leaping cheerfully up the chimney. He looked at her in surprise, as if he had indeed forgotten her.

'There was no reason why you should not ask for one,' he returned, unwinding his wet plaid before the fire. Her eyes widened.

'Have you forgotten so soon that I do not speak your language?'

He did not reply, merely looking at her in such a way that she wished she had not drawn his attention again to

that deficiency of hers. She crept a little nearer to the
warmth, and his eyes travelled to her bare legs and feet
beneath the shirt, and the curves of her body just visible
through it. She reached for the blanket to cover herself,
but he was already on the bed beside her. The intensity of his gaze set her blood pounding in her veins.
'Not again,' she thought. And: 'I was wrong. It is not
over.'

She felt his hair wet against her cheek, his mouth cool
on her lips, as his hands found their way beneath the
borrowed shirt, and she forgot her misery and her
loneliness. The feeble protest of her mind faded and
died and the fire leapt through her as Hector thrust her
back against the pillow.

Afterwards, she hated herself even as she lay warm
and contented, and watched him turn coldly away, his
body satisfied. Calmly, without emotion, he laid the
plaids to dry before the fire and dressed in shirt and trews
and tied back his hair. The rain had ceased now, and a
faint sunset light filled the room. He went to the window
and glanced out before moving towards the door.

'Don't leave me again!' Isobel cried out, sitting up. He
turned, eyebrows raised quizzically.

'Why ever not? Do you find my company so agree-
able?'

'No,' she returned, and saw him smile at her candour.
'But . . . but you left me all day, and I don't know what
to do, or where to go. You tell me nothing.'

'What is there to tell?' he returned impatiently, one
hand still on the door handle. 'I have my work to do, and
you have yours. You have been married before. You
must know what is expected of a wife.' He turned away,
adding as he opened the door:

'They will bring you supper before long.' And then he
stood still.

A great shout reached them from somewhere outside,
a shout filled with warning and excitement and triumph.
Voices answered from below, and Hector ran to the
window, thrusting it open. He called down questioning-
ly, and at the reply gave a joyful exclamation and ran

from the room leaving the window swinging wildly in the breeze.

Isobel drew a plaid—still damp—about her and followed him, consumed with curiosity. An air of expectancy hung over the castle, as if something incredible, wonderful was about to happen. Clansmen came running from all directions towards the main door. Isobel was swept along by their eagerness into the open, on to a level grassy space below the castle. They crowded together in silence, eyes on the mountainside, and she followed their gaze to a point high up, just below the summit.

There, a light glowed in the dusk against the black of the hillside. A moving light, coming steadily nearer, flickering and dancing like a fire. A strange light, formed of flames in the shape of a cross—

The clansmen were silent, motionless, but she could sense the excitement, the tension which linked them. The light drew nearer, and they could make out dimly the shadowy figure of the runner who carried it, borne triumphantly above his head like a banner. And as he came within earshot he called to them in Gaelic.

The tension snapped in a torrent of cheering. Hector turned, his face alight with joy, and seized Isobel about the waist and swung her off her feet and into the air.

'Isobel—Isobel—it is the fiery cross—the Prince has come!'

CHAPTER
SIX

'The Prince has come.'

So it had happened, the terrible thing they had all dreaded for so long. The flame of rebellion kindled again in the Highlands to sweep down on the peace and prosperity of the south bringing pillage and havoc and rapine, leaving the scars of a lingering fear long after it had been quenched.

And then Isobel recollected with a strange sensation that she was herself now linked in marriage to those terrible Highlanders, a part of them. The worst had already happened to her. She could have nothing more to fear, she could even hope, just a little, that the failure of the rebellion might bring her freedom. But at what cost?

She thought of her parents and all those she loved, still unsuspecting as yet of what was to come. And then she glanced round at the faces about her, and they seemed disfigured with blood-lust and battle fever, the long hatred of the Lowlander brought to horrible life. A chill shudder went through her.

Her coolness communicated itself even to Hector, elated though he was. Abruptly, he released her and said curtly: 'Go to your room—I will come. This is men's work,' and then stepped forward, forgetting her, to greet the approaching runner.

Isobel did not dare to disobey. Nor did she wish to linger any longer among these men made drunk on emotions as primitive and ancient as the mountains and shoreline of this wild land. She slipped away and ran quickly to the sanctuary of the bedroom, closing the door behind her, as if she could somehow shut out the scene she had witnessed.

The room was quiet and orderly, reassuringly civil-ised. Again she was struck by the contrast between Hector the barbarian chieftain at whose hands she had suffered, and the man who had, supposedly, left some-thing of himself imprinted on this room.

It was almost dark now, and she crossed to the table to light the candles which stood beside the mirror. Her own face gazed eerily back at her, lit by the flickering flames, the eyes wide and dark with fear of the unknown.

She had thought before that the future held unfore-seeable terrors, but she saw now that they were nothing against what might now lie ahead. For at least until today she had been certain that somewhere her parents and friends were alive and well and prospering, that something safe and normal lived on to reassure her that the whole world had not turned to chaos. Now there was no longer any certainty or safety.

She was still sitting before the mirror when Hector came in. He seemed almost feverish with excitement, moving restlessly about the room as he talked, the words tumbling out one over the other, his eyes bright, his hands gesturing eagerly.

'We have dreamed of this moment all through the years, Isobel. And now he is here—he landed two days ago, and the call has gone out.'

'Was that what the fiery cross meant? The sign to call you out?' put in Isobel.

Hector nodded. 'It is the ancient call to war of our people. We shall not hesitate. We leave at dawn—'

A cry broke from Isobel.

'At dawn!' She did not know quite why she was so dismayed. Hector nodded and came to stand beside her, taking her hands in his.

'You are my wife, so you must try to understand,' he said, his face alight, imploring, as she had never known it to be before. 'Our Prince has come, to lead us to war against the German Usurper in England. We shall rise to sweep him from the throne and bring to his inheritance our rightful King, our wronged King James. Thirty years we have waited, and prayed, and hoped and planned, and now the call has come. Are we now to say "not yet—give us two days more—give us time"? No, Isobel, when the call comes we follow, without fear or doubt or hesitation. Our Prince awaits us, on our own dear soil.'

'But,' Isobel returned, her voice hesitant, slow, against the lilting outpouring of his words, 'last time the rising failed, completely. The leaders were executed. It did not even seem that it might have succeeded, so I have been told. What makes you think it will be different this time?'

'Because we shall make it different!' Hector replied, his fervour unquenched. 'Every man who hesitates, who preaches caution, who fears failure—every timid spirit—threatens our enterprise, but every man who casts fear and doubt behind him and answers the call is worth ten of those others. It is not for us to ask if we shall succeed, but to go because we must. And we shall win, Isobel, this time we shall win. The Prince is young and brave—not like his father—he can lead us to victory.'

Looking into those burning eyes Isobel almost believed him. The Highlanders would be confronted by trained and seasoned troops, some of the best in Europe, her father said. But those troops did not know the Highlands as Hector did, they were not fired by ancient traditions of loyalty and honour, they had not the fierce warlike spirit of the men she had seen outside this evening. It would be like the setting of one way of life against another, the centuries-old fabric of the clans, bound by blood and loyalty, against the disciplined order of the modern army. In the Highlands the old ways might have the victory. But to restore the Old Pretender—King James—to his throne the rebels must march south, far from their familiar hills, to the Lowlands, and England, and at last to London.

And in their path, whatever the outcome, they would carry the war with them. Isobel shivered.

'Let me go home,' she said in a whisper.

For a moment Hector gazed at her blankly, as if he did not understand her. She had broken into his dream of glory and victory with her poor little request, and he

could not immediately take it in. And then the fire died
in his eyes, and he withdrew his hands and turned away.

'You will be safer here,' he said, without warmth. She
could see that she had offended him.

'I know,' she replied steadily. 'But if my parents are in
danger then I want to be with them.'

He faced her, his brows frowning sharply.

'You are my wife,' he reminded her. 'Your place is
here.'

'Not by choice,' said Isobel. 'How can you expect me
to be moved by an appeal of that kind? I owe you
nothing—except hatred, perhaps, for what you have
done to me.'

'I have given you my name,' he retorted angrily, and
Isobel laughed out loud.

'Do you really think I should be grateful for that?' she
demanded. Even as she posed the question she saw that
he did indeed think something of the kind. Amazingly,
he held her in such contempt that he thought he had
done her some kind of honour in abducting her and
forcing her into a coldly calculated marriage with a
Highlander of his birth and rank. Her eyes widened
as the truth dawned on her, and then she flared into
anger.

'How can you be so arrogant! You think you're God's
gift to mankind because you're born a Highlander. Let
me tell you that to any right-thinking person a Highlander is a thief and a barbarian and the lowest scum of the
earth.'

His hand flew up as if to strike her, and she recoiled
sharply. But the hand fell harmlessly to his side, though
he stood breathing quickly with anger, his eyes sparkling.

'A Highlander does not strike a woman,' he said
stiffly, as if it cost him a superhuman effort to abide by
that principle. 'But nor does he readily forget insults.
Remember that, though you are my wife. And tell me,'
he went on, a little more calmly, 'what is so virtuous
about the Lowlander, whose way of life is devoted to the
getting and spending of money, by fair means or foul?

To my people there are higher aims for which to live.'

'Have you forgotten why you married me?' asked Isobel acidly.

'Exactly,' he returned quickly. 'It is for those higher aims that I did so. For love of my people, to give them the means to live, not in luxury and soft comfort, but simply to live and grow strong. Because what we have is good and sweet and must be cherished above all.'

'Even at the cost of stealing cattle—and women—and of murder? Oh, I've heard all about your ways, Hector. John Campbell has chosen to turn his back on your fine Highland principles, but he remembers what he has left behind, and he has told me something of it.'

She saw her words had struck home, for the colour rose in his cheeks.

'Do not dare to speak that name under this roof or I shall indeed strike you!' he threatened.

'John Campbell is a good man,' Isobel returned defiantly. She saw his hands clench, and kept her eyes on them, warily.

'*Dhia*!' he exclaimed, as if the restraint was unbearable. And then he drew a deep breath, and seemed to recollect himself. 'We are wasting time, Isobel. Let us leave it. There is enough to be done before dawn.'

'Then may I not go home?' she asked again.

'No, damn you, woman, you may not!' he shouted. 'Your place is here, and here you shall remain until we return. And I expect from you all the dutiful submission of a wife who waits for her husband. You will remember the name you bear, and honour it. If you do not, then I shall hear of it.'

'So you set your clansmen to act as spies?' she asked. 'Is that also part of the fine honourable Highland way of life?'

'Don't taunt me, woman. Remember only that I shall be revenged, if I find cause enough.'

She shivered at the menace in his tone, but kept her head high and hoped that he saw only defiance in her eyes.

Isobel slept very little that night. She was relieved that

Hector allowed her to go to bed and that her wifely
duties did not seem to extend to helping the clan to
prepare for armed rebellion. She had no wish at all to be
a part of that. But once in bed she had small hope of
resting.

All night the bustle of preparation continued without
ceasing. Voices called, feet ran up and down stairs,
weapons clattered, ponies whinnied and dogs barked.
Now and then Hector came in to take something from
the chest or the cupboard and carry it downstairs. He did
not waste time in speaking to her, or even looking her
way.

It was not until after midnight that she fell asleep at
last, and it seemed as if her eyes had only that moment
closed when Hector's hand was on her shoulder, shaking
her awake.

'Come, Isobel, it is time.'

It was still dark, and the candles burned on the table.
Spread over the chair was Hector's plaid, and resting
against it the great sword she had seen in the chest and
the round leather-covered shield from the cupboard.
Hector wore shirt and trews and a tartan jacket, and his
hair was tied back with unaccustomed neatness. His
tingling excitement reached her at once.

'Come, help me make ready,' he commanded.

She scrambled yawning from the bed and dressed in
the inevitable plaid, and then came obediently to pin the
brooch which secured his own plaid. Now, as he was
about to set out on the greatest adventure of his life,
Hector wanted his wife to carry out the small duties
which any Highland wife would perform for her husband at such a time. He stood smiling slightly as she
buckled the sword belt about him, her fingers fumbling
at the unfamiliar task, and pulled the folds of the plaid to
lie at their most graceful across his shoulders, handed
him dirk and pistol to thrust in his belt, and then held out
the bonnet with its eagle's feather for him to take with a
quiet word of thanks. Then she stood back and looked at
him, seeing a stranger dressed for war. His magnificence
drew a reluctant admiration from her.

'Now to breakfast,' he said, linking her arm through his.

She felt strange as she left the room at his side, drawn into this elaborate drama, as the devoted wife parting with her heroic husband. His mood had caught her against her will, and she found herself playing her part with grave dignity. She was not sure if she did so because she was still half asleep or because she was afraid of what he might do if she refused to do as he asked. Whatever it was, she found herself unable to resist.

In the hall the clansmen were gathered, and the tables set with a simple breakfast. To Isobel's surprise many of the women were there, brought back some time during the night. But perhaps that was not so surprising, for they must love the men who were setting out on this enterprise of deadly danger. For them there would be no excitement, no longing for battle to rouse their spirits. Only fear, because they must know that their men were marching in open rebellion against all the might of England. And even in Ardshee, isolated by sea and mountain, they must know what that could mean.

Hector led her to the cold fireside, where old Mairi MacLean waited quietly, her son Hugh at her side. In her eyes Isobel read a pride and love so great that they veiled the fear lurking there. She would not show the two men who meant so much to her what it cost her to part with them. Briefly she glanced at Isobel, with a sudden warmth, as if to say 'Do as I do. Keep your dignity'. 'Does she really think I care what becomes of them all?' thought Isobel.

'My foster mother will remain here at the castle with you,' said Hector quietly. 'You will learn much from her.'

'So she is the spy,' thought Isobel, but she merely smiled coolly, and politely, at the old woman, and said nothing.

The men ate on their feet, as if their errand today was too urgent to be delayed by a leisurely meal. And as they ate the women brought food for the journey, oatmeal and cheese and bannocks, and then carried to husbands and brothers and fathers the white cockades which their chieftain distributed, the knot of white ribbon which marked their loyalty to King James. With shaking hands Isobel did as the other women, and pinned Hector's own cockade to his bonnet, with a sickening sense that this must, very likely, amount to treason.

At last Hector gave the command to leave and the clansmen moved towards the door, the women following.

In the bay the ship which had brought them here two days ago waited expectantly. For the first time Isobel noticed what an odd-looking vessel it was, storm-battered, high at stem and prow, with its single mast and long rows of oars. As strange and primitive as everything else at Ardshee.

On the shore the piper took up his position and began to play a solemn farewell. Women clung to their menfolk, children were lifted into their fathers' arms for a parting kiss. Hector turned to kneel for his foster-mother's blessing, and then embraced her.

Isobel looked away as he did so, for she could not bear to watch the tender little scene. It hurt her, emphasising her own isolation. 'Not,' she thought, 'that I want kindness from him. But it is hard to be loved by no one at all.'

Mairi MacLean released her foster-son at last, her eyes bright with tears she was too proud to shed, and held out her arms to Hugh. And then Hector took Isobel's hands in his, gravely, as if he wanted her to play out her part to the end.

'Isobel MacLean, let me be proud of the wife I have taken. Then one day there may be kindness between us. Mairi will care for you. Comfort and cherish her for your part. And have courage.'

He bent then, and she felt his mouth brush her forehead. No passion, no fire, simply a chaste farewell. She raised her eyes to his.

'Goodbye,' she said, because she could think of nothing else to say.

He released her hands and with a final call to his men

strode towards the water. They carried him on their
shoulders through the waves, and then Isobel saw him
swing himself over the side and onto the ship. The men
scrambled after him.

Later, when, oars flashing in the early sun, the ship
slid out of the bay to the open water beyond and spread
her sail to catch the breeze, Isobel saw Hector in the
prow, his face turned unwaveringly to the shore. And
she knew that it was not on her small solitary figure he
gazed, as she stood a little apart from the other women;
but at the line of mountain and wood and castle, and the
brave figures of those others who remained behind. It
was there his heart lay, with this land and its people, and
it was with them his thoughts would linger through the
perilous weeks to come.

CHAPTER
SEVEN

LONG after the ship had sailed beyond the headland, and the first sunlight had stretched long fingers into the bay, the watchers stood there, gazing out over the empty water. And then, without a sign or a word, they began in ones and twos to drift away. The sounds of daily life, the crying of a baby, a voice calling to the hens, the clatter as pots were scoured, had already begun to rise in the stillness when Isobel felt her arm taken and heard old Mairi MacLean speak softly to her in Gaelic.

She turned sharply, stung out of the numbing chill which had descended upon her as the boat sailed away. The little drama was over, and her part with it. And she realised with deadly suddenness that Hector had left her to an isolation more terrible than total solitude. Only he amongst all his people spoke English: and he had gone. She felt a fierce desire to burst into tears. She longed to run into the woods and find some quiet place where she could give way to all her unhappiness unobserved. But Mairi MacLean, Hector's spy, was at her side, holding her arm, urging her towards the castle. Isobel bit her trembling lip and allowed the old woman to lead her back along the shady path.

In the hall of the castle Isobel turned automatically towards the stair leading to her bedroom. There, perhaps, Mairi would leave her by herself. Her own company would be better far than that of all these people to whom she could not speak, who could not hope to bring her any comfort. But to her astonishment the gnarled fingers tugged at her arm, holding her back as she reached out to open the door. She turned her head, eyes wide.

Mairi tugged again, and gestured towards the tables

still laden with the debris of that hurried breakfast.

'She wants me to help clear up,' Isobel realised, suddenly rebellious. Why should she? It was servants' work, and she owed these people nothing. Angrily, she shook her head, and pulled herself free from the restraining hand.

She had escaped as far as the door, and had it open, when Mairi caught up with her. She had an eager look, as if she were offering some pleasant choice to Isobel. In her hand, now, she held a piece of cheese. Isobel looked down, puzzled, as the old woman stretched out her palm, as if offering the cheese to a horse.

'*Càise*,' she said urgently, pointing with her free hand to the cheese. '*Càise.*'

Isobel wrinkled her brow again, shrugged, turned to go, one foot on the first stair. The old woman pointed to herself.

'Mairi,' she said. Then, taking Isobel's hand, laid it over the cheese. '*Càise*,' she repeated again.

Isobel retraced the one step she had taken towards freedom, and faced Mairi. Understanding began to dawn on her. Was *càise* the Gaelic word for cheese? She waited and, sensing that she had Isobel's attention at last, Mairi touched her shoulder.

'*Iseabal*,' she said, in a musical version of the girl's own name. And then, pointing again in turn to herself and the cheese: 'Mairi—*càise*.'

She smiled then, and took Isobel's hand to lead her back towards the untidy tables.

Isobel was intrigued. So Mairi wanted her to learn some words of Gaelic, to try and break through the barrier that cut her off from those about her? Was that Hector's idea, his parting instruction to her, or had some sympathy for Isobel's plight told her that this was a practical way to help?

Then resentment overcame her surprise and curiosity. Hector had gone, to take part in a rebellion of which she could only heartily disapprove. She was deserted, far from home and friends and all that was familiar. She had suffered terrible wrongs at the hands of Hector and his people. All she wanted now was to be alone and weep. Why should she exert herself to learn the language of a people she hated and despised, why should she subdue her natural instinct to find relief in tears? She shook her head, fiercely, at the old woman and turned back towards the stairs.

And then she paused. After all, what point was there in tears? They could change nothing. She was here, a virtual prisoner, with no hope of escape. Even if by some miracle the failure of the rebellion brought her freedom and took her home again to her parents there would be weeks, months even, to live through in this place. Weary months, with no one to share her thoughts, to comfort her, few books to read, little to do. Better, surely, to find some occupation. And what more absorbing, more demanding in this uncivilised place than to set her mind to master this barbaric and yet oddly beautiful language?

She came back to Mairi's side and lifted a hunk of cheese from the table.

'*Càise*,' she said.

In the weeks that followed Isobel found to her surprise that she had a quick ear and an apt tongue for learning a language. And Mairi was a good teacher. Each day she would add a few more words to Isobel's growing vocabulary, whilst making sure that the words learned yesterday or the day before were carefully repeated. Soon, Isobel found that she could understand, now and then, something of the talk about her. And the moment when she greeted Hector's foster-mother in Gaelic as they met in the morning was one of real triumph, for both of them. She began to forget, very soon, that Mairi was Hector's spy, and a warm affection replaced the suspicion of the early days.

The language was not all she learned. Mairi took her to the shieling, and there taught her to milk the cows and goats, to make cheese, to wash and mend and cook. It was all so new, so far removed from her urban experience, that Isobel forgot it was 'servants' work' and even began to enjoy herself.

Slowly, imperceptibly, she became part of the
small community of women and girls, old men and
young boys, accepted, one of themselves. She slept
in a little hut at the shieling, ate in their company,
gathered with them in the evening for the singing
and talking and story-telling which went on far into the
night.

They had no news at all of how the men were faring so
far from home. Hector might almost never have existed,
if his foster-mother had not talked of him, now and then,
when she and Isobel were alone. There were tales of his
childhood, of the long days when he and Hugh played
barefoot and happy in glen and mountain, fishing and
hunting, minding the cattle with the other boys, swimming and wrestling. And there were tales of Hector the
Chieftain caring for his people, respected and loved as a
father and brother, who wanted their well-being above
all.

Late in September the days grew short and squally
storms blew over from the sea. The turf huts which had
sheltered them all summer long were abandoned to the
vagaries of the weather, the cattle and goats and delicate
silken-coated sheep herded together and driven down to
the sparser pasturage near the castle. Cooking pots,
tools, the few clothes, the simple bedding, were
gathered up and carried back to the settlement on the
shore. Fires were lit on the raised stone hearths of the
little houses, and smoke curled its way in a desultory
manner through the ragged heather thatch, scenting the
air with the acrid fragrance of burning peat. Isobel
returned to the castle, and Mairi took up residence in her
own small room beside the hall.

On the cliff face the trees turned to fiery gold and
bronze and copper, as if the woods were ablaze. Sometimes in the mornings mist lay on the sea, lifting hazily
about midday to let in a dusty golden sunlight. All day
the people, young and old, worked in the little fields low
on the hillside by the settlement, gathering in the poor
and weed-ridden crops of oats and barley. Their singing,
keeping time with the swish and bite of the sickle on the

partly-ripened stems, echoed around the little bay and
filled the daylight hours.

When it was too wet to work outdoors the women sat
in the crowded one-roomed houses with the chickens
roosting on the roof beams and the children playing in
the mud at their feet. Hands busy with distaff and
spindle, they spun the yarn for the winter plaids from
wool dyed with plants and roots gathered from shore and
hillside and woodland. Isobel learned their skills and
made soft shoes for herself from deerskin, and a blue
woollen gown. With Mairi's help she wove a fine plaid to
drape around it, and the old woman murmured the
customary blessing over it before she put it on.

Often after dark the people came to the castle, for the
ceilidh—the gathering for singing and story telling—for
there was more space there than in the single cramped
rooms of the little houses.

It was on just such an evening that they were raising
their voices in a favourite song of light-hearted love,
when the deerhounds suddenly leapt up from their
somnolent position at Isobel's feet and ran wildly barking towards the main door.

The singing faded at once, dying away to a silence
broken only by the clamour of the dogs and the hiss of a
damp log on the fire. It was raining tonight, but it was the
soft insistent soundless rain which Isobel had come to
realise was only too usual at Ardshee.

Then they heard what had aroused the dogs. Steps,
and voices, approached the castle, just beyond the
closed door. Isobel stood up, and Mairi with her. Fear of
the unknown gripped them, for they knew that all the
clan, young and old, were here with them. The door
opened—and the dogs, as suddenly quiet, bounded out
with delightedly waving tails.

Hector and Hugh stepped into the hall.

There was a moment of complete silence, and then
Mairi gave a great joyful exclamation. She hurried to
them to embrace first one and then the other and bring
them to the fire. And then Hector stood before Isobel,
and she experienced that strange, forgotten lurch deep

inside her as his dark eyes met hers. She felt her colour
rise under his gaze, but said quietly, through quickened
breathing:

'You are welcome, man of the house.' She did not
realise she had spoken in Gaelic, for she had grown used
to speaking nothing else. For a moment, too, Hector
only gazed at her, and then took her hands in his.

'Thanks be to you, woman of the house,' he replied in
the same language. His voice too sounded oddly breathless, a little unsteady.

At last he wrenched his eyes from her as if with an
effort and turned to greet the others. And it was then
that he paused, eyes wide, and gave a small gasp of
astonishment.

'What did you say?' he asked in English. Isobel was
astonished at how strange and unfamiliar the words
sounded.

She repeated her greeting, her colour deepening still
more, and saw him smile warmly, with real delight, as
Mairi explained how she had passed the time in his
absence. At the end of the old woman's account he
reached out and drew Isobel into his arms and kissed
her long and tenderly. That sweet melting of the
limbs flowed through her, and she held him close, her
fingers looped in his springing hair. If they had been
alone—

But they were not alone, and the waiting throng was
hungry for news. Hector gently put her from him,
though he retained her hand, and gave his attention to
the women who had no men to welcome.

The news, for all of them, was amazing, wonderful,
almost too good to be true. The Highlanders had risen
impressively—if not quite to a man—to support their
Prince. Now after a bare two months of fighting almost
the whole of Scotland, but for one or two isolated
garrisons, lay in their hands. Just a few days ago, at
Prestonpans near Edinburgh, they had gained a magnificent victory against government troops. Now it only
remained for them to gather all their strength for the
march on England. There, the Prince had been assured,

his Jacobite supporters would rise and the opposition melt away like mist with the sun.

Best of all, every man who had left Ardshee on that summer morning was alive and well and enjoying a well earned rest in Edinburgh. Hector and Hugh, their chieftain explained vaguely, had returned on a small but urgent matter of business and would stay a day, perhaps two, before setting out again for the glorious end to the adventure.

After that, the singing and dancing and stories and poetry flowed as they never had before. Whisky was brought out, and chickens roasted, and the piper's small son played merry tunes on the little pipe on which he practised his father's craft. Isobel sat quietly, her eyes on Hector, noting how his appearance bore out his words, for he looked like a man who had seen victory, and knew he would see it again. Happy, relaxed, his eyes glowing in his tanned face, he lent his voice to the singing with deep fervour. And now and then he looked her way, and his eyes seemed to be sending her warm and tender messages, so full of meaning that a shiver of anticipatory delight ran down her spine.

At long last the company took their leave, and Hector and Isobel were left alone, facing each other across the fireside.

'I am thinking,' whispered Hector softly, 'that it is bed time, my wife.'

Again that delighted shiver. She put her hand in his and went with him, soft-footed, up the winding stair to their room. There, with great care, he gently closed the door, and then turned to her. He undid the brooch from her plaid—the smaller plaid Mairi had made—and let the tartan folds fall to the floor. Then his strong slender fingers set neatly to work on the lacings of the gown, and the petticoat. And then he carried her, wild with desire, to the bed.

He knelt at her side, and brushed the corn-gold hair from her forehead, and whispered:

'My wife,' in a voice as caressing as his hand, as it made its exquisite way over her smooth tingling skin.

And then he made love to her as he had never done before, with a consuming passion that yet held a lingering tenderness, answering the flame of her desire with a sweet generosity which was entirely, delightfully new. This time, when at last he drew back, she felt no shame, no dismay, only a blissful happiness, a drowsy contentment.

Nor did Hector simply turn away, his body satisfied. Instead he lay beside her, leaning on one arm, running his finger with idle tenderness down her cheek.

'Wife of my heart,' he said softly, and it struck her how well suited the Gaelic was to words of love. 'You have pleased me more than I can say. You are indeed worthy to bear my name.'

The first cloud slid between them. Isobel felt a quiver of irritation that even at this moment his pride in his name was still uppermost in his mind. But she smiled, saying nothing. She did not want to break this new mood of tenderness.

'Do you know why I came back to Ardshee?' he went on. She shook her head lazily, still smiling. Would he say: 'because of you'?

'To take you back with me,' he said, and she thought that she had almost been right, though the words startled her.

'Back with you?' she repeated. 'Back where?'

'To Edinburgh, first,' he said. 'For a little while we shall remain there, to allow more men to come in. There will be balls and merry-making. Many wives have come to be with their husbands, and I should like to have you, too, at my side. Let the world see that you have honoured me with your hand, and that we have found joy together.'

'You have honoured me.' That, Isobel thought, was a new way for him to look at their marriage. Until now— even a moment ago—he had made it clear that all the honour had been for him to give. She felt elated, happy at the prospect of company, and balls, new clothes perhaps, and—

'Perhaps I could see my parents. It is not far,' she said

eagerly, and then wondered with a little chill if she had said too much.

But Hector only smiled the more warmly.

'That too, my heart. We shall meet them together, so that they will know you are in good hands.' She was a little doubtful as to whether they would be so easily convinced, but she said nothing.

'Then,' Hector went on casually, avoiding her gaze, 'they will know that they can safely entrust your fortune to me.'

CHAPTER
EIGHT

A CHILL fell on Isobel's spirit like a winter frost. The last vestiges of contentment, the budding happiness within her, shrivelled and died. The full implication of Hector's words worked its way steadily to her heart, leaving bitterness in its path.

What a fool she was! Just for a short while she had thought he cared for her a little, that his pride in her achievements, his admiration for her beauty, had kindled some real affection in him. That ardent love-making with its new gentleness had seemed to promise a true flowering between them.

And now she knew that it had all been a ruse. She had been told that Highlanders were sly, not to be trusted. Hector had proved that even in their most secret moments it was true. The thought that he could lightly make a pretence of passion and love to gain his ends was devastating, shattering. All that tenderness, for money!

The momentary chill gave way to a fierce consuming anger. She pushed his caressing hand away, recoiled from him, began quickly, furiously, to dress.

'You are a snake!' she hissed. 'A poisonous, slimy, vile snake! That was all you wanted, nothing else, all this time. I hate and loathe and detest you more than I can ever say. Go back to your Prince, and I hope they hang you as a vile rebel and leave your bones to rot and the birds to pick out your eyes!'

She spoke in English, but her words had all the venom of the Gaelic curses Hector knew from the old tales. She saw him whiten, and for a moment thought her anger had struck him as surely as any blow. And then his mouth tightened, and the colour rose in his cheeks and

his eyes shone with a deadly light. He leapt from the bed,
and she shrank back against the panelling, breathing fast
with fear, yet holding her head defiantly.

This time he did strike her, sharply, on the cheek.

'That is a warning, wife!' he snarled. 'Insult me again
and there will be worse, far worse!'

Isobel tossed her head.

'Do your worst!' she said. 'I'm not your slave or your
chattel. Everything you do only puts you further in the
wrong. One day you'll answer for it, and then you'll wish
every word and deed undone. Get away from me. I wish
to dress.'

His fingers closed inexorably about her wrist, and
against her will his eyes held hers.

'You will do as I wish,' he said in a cold soft voice,
deadly with menace. 'You will come with me and act the
dutiful wife, and take me when I ask to visit your parents
and show them how happy you are. And you will bring
your fortune to me, every single penny of it.'

'And what if I do not?' she demanded, only with a
great effort keeping the tremor from her voice.

'I shall be at your side, Isobel, every moment of every
day and all night long. And Hugh will be at your other
side. And there are many secret ways to die.'

She shivered, and swallowed hard.

'What will you do when you have the money?' she
taunted him, though her voice sounded cracked and
unnatural. 'Spend it on the whores of Edinburgh?'

She saw his free hand move up as if to strike again, but
he thought better of it.

'Foul-mouthed bitch!' The words had all the force of a
blow. 'It is no business of yours what I do with it.'

'It is my money!' she exclaimed indignantly.

'And you are my wife. Everything you are, and all you
have, is mine by right and duty.' He saw the flame light
her eyes as she opened her mouth to speak, and realised
he would not reach her that way. His voice took on a less
strident, faintly pleading note: 'Isobel, the Prince has
need of your money. We march on England, and supplies are low. The men need food, and arms. We were

promised French support, and it has not come. Your
wealth could mean so much.'

'So that's it!' she cried, illumination dawning. 'You
want my money to finance your treasonable rebellion
against your lawful King. I have never been anything but
a loyal and true servant of our good King George II, and
I don't intend to begin now. The only possible outcome I
pray for and long for—the only thing I'd give my money
for—is that your pretty Princeling should go back into
exile and stay there. He and his family have brought
nothing but trouble on this land for over a hundred
years. It's time it was brought to an end, for good and
all.'

'What can you possibly know about it?' he sneered.

'I have ears, and a brain, and a father who thought
long about these things, and talked about them with me.
Just because you forced me into marriage and possessed
me with your body does not mean that you have my mind
and heart prisoner too. Whatever you do to me, Hector
MacLean, I am free of you, free to think as I choose.
And you shall not lay hands on one penny of my money.'

Burning with frustration at her clear-eyed defiance, he
took her by the shoulders and shook her until her teeth
rattled.

'You will do as I say, woman!'

'If I come to Edinburgh,' she returned quietly, when
at last he was still, 'I shall make it only too plain what you
have done to me and what I think of you. And I shall tell
nothing but the plain truth to my parents. And if you kill
me, well then you will still not lay your hands on the
money, nor will you any longer be able to hope that you
may have it one day.'

His hands fell to his sides, and he stood gazing at her in
silence, acknowledging her triumph. She thought, even,
that she saw a trace of a grudging admiration in his eyes.
She knew she had won.

Hector's next remark, spoken in a low despondent
tone, full of weariness and regret, took her by surprise.

'Then there is no hope for us,' he said, and turned
away from her.

Without another word, or a glance in her direction, he dressed quickly and left the room, closing the door firmly but quietly behind him. The click of the latch had an odd note of finality which brought a new and unaccountable chill to Isobel's heart.

After a little while she undressed again and went to bed. She felt overwhelmingly tired after her long defiance: it had cost her far more than she had realised at the time to meet his threats with courage and anger. But sleep eluded her for a large part of the night. She felt depressed, downcast by all that had happened. It was the harder to bear because of the little flower of hope which had blossomed on Hector's return. At least, though, she was no longer afraid. Some instinct told her that Hector had already done his worst and, having found it a failure, would at least leave her alone in future. It was some comfort.

A storm blew up some time during the night. The wind howled wildly about the castle, hurling rain like stones at the small windows. The roar of the waves on the rocky shore outdid even the wind. In an odd way, Isobel found, the sound of the tempest was soothing, belittling the trivial disagreements of the human beings sheltered within these stone walls. She fell asleep at last with the crash of the sea like a lullaby in her ears.

Mairi woke her soon after dawn, coming into the room with a sad mouth and reproach in her eyes. Isobel was struck for the first time at how her gaunt features resembled Hugh's. Clearly he took after her. But it was her foster-son who was uppermost in her mind at present.

'You have angered him,' said Mairi sadly, without other greeting, standing at the foot of the bed. Isobel felt a twinge of guilt, and then repressed it. She was surely not to blame that she would not allow Hector to use her as callously as if she were an inanimate object.

'I'm sorry,' she said, untruthfully, but wanting to regain Mairi's approval. She sensed that the old woman blamed her for the rift. 'I did not choose to anger him, but it happened that way. Perhaps you can help us to be friends again.' It was a forlorn hope in the circumstances, but she thought it might console Mairi.

Mairi shook her head and said:

'It is too late. My sons have gone.'

At that Isobel sat bolt upright, her eyes wide.

'Gone? But when? Hector said nothing—and the storm—!' She thought of the waves lashing on the rocks and shivered. For all her anger she did not really wish him to be battered to death on his native shore.

'They went before the storm,' said Mairi. She hesitated, rubbing the folds of the bed curtain between her fingers, eyes lowered. Isobel realised she was trying to find words to convey something unpleasant. She felt a little twinge of fear.

At last Mairi raised her head, drawing a deep breath as if gathering strength.

'My foster-son gave orders that you are to remain here in this room,' she said without emotion.

Isobel was puzzled.

'What do you mean, remain here? I never doubted that I was to do so. It has been my room since I came, except when we were at the shieling.'

'You are not to leave it,' Mairi explained, still in that same even tone.

Realisation hit Isobel like a blow in the stomach.

'Not to leave it? Not at all? You mean I am a prisoner?'

Mairi nodded, and said with difficulty: 'Yes, that is so. It is his wish.'

Isobel longed to leap from the bed and rage and stamp and shout in fury at the senseless vindictiveness of the order. What possible purpose could it serve, when she was in effect already a prisoner here? What possible purpose except to satisfy a mean, small-minded desire for revenge?

With an effort she controlled herself, though her eyes sparkled with anger, and said in a voice which only vibrated a little:

'I will not say what I think of that, because I respect

you. Did he tell you how long I was to stay here?'

'It will be until he returns,' explained Mairi, with audible regret. 'Whenever that is,' thought Isobel.

'I suppose I will be fed?' she asked aloud.

'You are to have a fire,' Mairi conceded, 'and food in plenty, and candles. And I may bear you company sometimes, if you wish.'

So he wanted her alive and well at least, thought Isobel grimly. It was a small crumb of comfort.

At times during that autumn, while the frequent storms shook the very rock on which the castle stood, or when the landscape was shrouded in a chill sea mist, Isobel did not find her imprisonment irksome. She would not then in any case have wished to be outside. She was warm and well-fed, she had books to read and sewing to do, and Mairi sat with her and told stories and talked of this and that, almost as in the days before Hector came home.

But when the sun shone warm on the browning bracken and the sea sparkled and the gulls floated free against the blue sky, Isobel paced the room restlessly and longed to be outside.

She missed the company of the other women, too, the ceilidhs, the laughter, the many everyday tasks made enjoyable because they were shared with friends. Most of all she regretted the change in Mairi.

The old woman treated her kindly, but Isobel knew that it would be a very long time before anything approaching the old ease and affection between them would return. However much she might sympathise with Isobel's plight, it was Hector who was first in Mairi's heart, as dearly loved as her own son. And if Isobel had offended him, for whatever reason, she could not quite be forgiven as long as his anger lasted.

It was fortunate that the years of her first marriage had taught Isobel patience above all else. Without that hard-earned lesson she did not think she could have faced so calmly the long and irksome imprisonment. As it was, she had long ago found that she had resources within her to endure solitude and confinement, if she

chose to draw on them. The hardest part now was not the
lack of freedom, but a constant ache of sadness, like a
leaden weight about her heart, which seemed to have
settled there since Hector left. She could not quite
explain it, but she learned in time to live with it.

It was a quite unforeseen event which overturned her
composure at last. It should not have been unforeseen at
all, but the fact that she had escaped it so far had lulled
Isobel into a false sense of security which was to be
rudely shattered.

She realised she was going to have a child.

At first the realisation struck her like a sudden cold
shower, depriving her of any will to react. She said
nothing to Mairi, explaining away an early bout of
sickness as an upset occasioned by eating doubtful fish
the night before. Slowly, another kind of nausea troubled her, settling deep inside her, fed by fear. For this
new, strange, portentous thing had happened while she
was far from home, estranged from the man responsible,
a helpless prisoner.

In the end, after two days, Mairi noticed the shadows
sleeplessness had left about her eyes and decided that
the sickness could be no coincidence. She took Isobel's
hand in hers and asked her bluntly if she were to be the
mother of Hector's child.

Isobel nodded dumbly, not much liking the way the
question was worded. But Mairi had fostered Hector, so
to her it must be almost as if she were to be a grand-
mother. Her joy was instant, and transparent.

'Then we must take every care of you,' she exclaimed
delightedly. 'You must have the best food—and fresh
air, when the weather is fine. A gentle walk: I shall go
with you. I think that would be Hector's wish—'

Isobel allowed the talk to flow round her, taking little
in. Instead, her mind dwelt on the knowledge that she
would have to bear her child according to the unknown,
alien ways of the clan. She had shared the life of the
people through the summer, and been happy. But this
was different, and she was dreadfully afraid. Childbirth,
she knew, was a dangerous and painful business. She

longed suddenly for the reassuring, totally dependable love of her mother. Surely at such a time this was what a woman needed above all?

A further realisation hit her as Mairi helped her into her warmest plaid and they ventured out into the crisp sunlight of the early winter day. Here at Ardshee, even if she survived the birth, even if all went as well as could be, the child would not be her own. What was it Hector had said? 'The son of the chieftain is always fostered until he is twelve or so with a woman of the clan.' They would take the child from her, put it in the arms of another young woman with small children of her own. And she would see him only at a distance, growing up in another home, away from her care and her love. Unless, she supposed, the baby was a girl. But even then she was not sure. She knew so little of the customs by which she would be forced to live.

Despair clutched at her heart so that she scarcely noticed how sweet the air was after her long incarceration. She had never in all the past months longed so much as she did now for the dear familiarity of her home. She was amazed that it could ever have seemed unreal. It was this life which was unreal, walking on a foreign shore with the waves lapping at her feet and this uncouth garment shrouding her body. If willpower had been all that was needed she would have dived into the icy water and swum and swum until she reached safety and freedom. Only it was not enough, and she could not swim.

There was nothing for it but to endure.

CHAPTER
NINE

Now that Isobel was to bear Hector's child, Mairi for-
gave her everything. The old warmth returned between
them, tempered only by Isobel's longing for home,
which cut her off a little from everything at Ardshee.
Gradually, Mairi relaxed her guard on the girl, feeling
that in the circumstances even the unforgiving Hector
would not want to carry revenge so far.

Winter had set in with frosts and storms and bitter
winds. It was not often that Isobel wished to venture far
from the fireside and Mairi's attentive company. At
times, though, the old woman's enthusiasm for the
prospect which so terrified her grew too much for her
and she would go out to walk briskly along the shore,
finding relief in the fierce power of wind and spray.

There was no further news from the absent clansmen.
Patiently, rarely talking of the rebellion, the women
carried on their daily lives as if nothing had changed.
During the brief hours of daylight they toiled laborious-
ly, fingers reddened and sore with cold, and after dark
they huddled about the peat fires and found comfort in
song and story.

It was during the shortest winter days, when the light
seemed a fugitive thing, scarcely breaking through the
darkness before night came again, that Isobel found
herself wandering further along the shore than she had
ever done before. Deep in gloomy thoughts, she followed the narrow shingly beach eastward from the bay,
away from the castle.

It was colder than ever today, grey and cheerless, and
even Hector's plaid wound over the blue woollen gown
did little to protect her from the wind. She thrust
numbed fingers into the tartan folds and plodded dog-

gedly on. She was not sure what she was thinking, only that she was desperately miserable, longing for some miracle to bring her hope for the future.

Unseeing, she scrambled over a rocky outcrop, and into another bay. Here the trees came to an end, and a steep grassy slope ran up from shore to skyline. Only a tiny huddle of pines at the far side of the bay broke its smooth line before the cliffs rose again, daunting and impenetrable. Isobel paused, coming briefly back to the present, and gazed across the little bay.

On the shore a small boat was drawn up above the tide line, oars laid neatly together inside it.

She glanced quickly around. There was no sign of life. But someone must have brought the boat there. It was a small wooden boat, without a sail, and she knew it could not have come from Ardshee. She crunched her way over the shingle to look at it.

She had almost reached the boat when a shout from somewhere in the woods a little above where she had been standing just now caught her attention. She turned her head, and saw a man emerge from the trees and run swiftly across the bay towards her, clearly angry. And his appearance struck her motionless with amazement.

This was no Highlander wild in plaid and bonnet, but a respectable gentleman dressed in powdered wig and neat snuff-coloured coat as if he had just stepped out of the streets of Edinburgh or Stirling. And as he came nearer she realised, her astonishment growing every moment, that she knew him.

John Campbell was running towards her, his face red with rage and exertion, crying out in English that she must keep her dirty hands from his boat.

She waited, quietly, pushing the plaid back a little from her face so that he should know her. And a few feet away he paused, his light blue eyes wondering, puzzled.

'Isobel?' he asked, uncertainly. 'Mrs Carnegie?'

'Not that any more,' she said quietly. 'I am Isobel MacLean now.'

She saw an angry light flicker somewhere in his eyes, and he swore under his breath. It was an extreme reaction for John, and it startled her. But he had himself under control in a moment, though his mouth was still held in a tight line.

'Not for much longer, my dear,' he said gently, coming closer. 'Not if it is within my power.' And he took her hands in his as she reached out to welcome him.

She saw his eyes travel over her, noting the unfamiliar clothes which had led him to take her for an inquisitive Highland girl. More than that, he was remembering her as he had last seen her, in her black widow's gown, her hair neat under its little silk cap, quiet, innocent, inexperienced.

The blue eyes which gazed at him now, warm with welcome, had seen a great deal since that summer day. This was no longer an untouched girl who stood before him, but a woman. A woman who had suffered much, but who had faced it all with courage and an unsuspected strength. And she looked well—not just well, he amended, but beautiful, more beautiful than ever. The colours of the tartan, barbaric though he thought them, emphasised the glowing rose and gold and blue of her skin and eyes. The hair falling in heavy shining waves beneath the folds of the plaid, unpinned, unadorned, was so springing with life that he longed to run his hands over it. The sweet-natured headstrong girl had become a lovely woman, glowing with vitality, for all the traces of unhappiness which still lingered below her welcoming smile.

She laughed suddenly, with surprise and pleasure.

'But I don't understand,' she said. 'How did you get here?'

Smiling, he indicated the boat.

'I crossed the loch,' he explained.

That puzzled her. 'What loch?'

He waved his hand towards the east.

'There, beyond that point. Did you not know there was a great sea loch running into the Sound just there? It almost cuts this godforsaken place off from the rest of the Scottish mainland.'

'You mean . . .' Her eyes widened. 'You mean this is

not an island? And all this time I could have run away and if I'd kept walking long enough I'd have reached home in the end?'

'You'd not have got far in these hills,' he assured her firmly. 'It's well enough for Highlanders, knowing their way about—though even they prefer to use the sea. Not,' he added, with an unfavourable glance at the grey water, 'that I can see that it's any safer that way.' He smiled with new gentleness, and drew her arm protectively through his, laying his hand over hers. 'But we must not waste time talking. I have come to take you home. We have a long journey ahead of us.'

'Home!' she breathed, tears rushing to her eyes. 'Oh, yes please—at once!'

He led her to where the boat stood, and helped her in. Then he thrust the boat onto the sea, jumped in, wetting his feet a little in the process, and took up the oars.

Even Isobel, no expert herself, could see that he had little experience of rowing. And it became clear very soon that John Campbell was mortally afraid of the vast expanse of grey water, full of hidden rocks and treacherous currents. But he was no coward, and he bent his head against the wind, and set his teeth, and rowed doggedly if unevenly towards the distant line of mountains which marked the point where the loch he had spoken of met the sea.

Isobel did not find John's obvious terror very reassuring, but it moved her deeply that he should have come to seek her in spite of it. She recognised, with humility, what it must have cost him, and knew it was a measure of his affection for her.

As the boat rocked and tossed its way over the waves John tried to take his mind from his fear by telling her, rather breathlessly, how he had come to find her.

By some amazing coincidence he had met one day with an acquaintance who had, briefly, been a prisoner of the Highland rebels. And that man had told in passing how he had heard talk of Ardshee's new and wealthy bride. So, struck by a wild hope, saying nothing to her parents, John had set out in search of that bride.

'And so,' John ended, 'here I am. I thought that if I landed on the coast a little way from Ardshee I might be able to watch the place unobserved, and see if you were there. It was pure chance which brought you walking this way.'

'But a very lucky one,' added Isobel, thankfully.

In spite of John's worst fears, and his rowing, they reached the coast in safety, and he took her first to the home of a relative to rest and eat.

A long and uncomfortable journey on the rough and narrow Highland roads followed, enlivened only by John Campbell's attentive and reassuring presence. He answered her eager questions about her parents, how they were well and how, mercifully, the rebellion had largely passed them by. Not that it was over yet, but the rebels had crossed into England some weeks ago, and with luck they would not return.

'The English won't let them off as lightly as our spineless generals have done,' John asserted, though Isobel thought he did not sound entirely convinced.

Clearly the rebellion had already been a good deal more successful than had been expected. And if the English, only lukewarm in their enthusiasm for their Hanoverian King, should decide to side with the charming young man who led the invasion—but then, John added, that charming young man was a Catholic, and the English hated Papists more than they disliked a foreign King whose unedifying family quarrels were public knowledge.

Isobel was not sure if his words comforted her. She found that she could not entirely share his fervent wish for the defeat of the rebels. Yet she was a loyal subject of King George, as she had told Hector. Perhaps she was troubled by the thought of all the women and children who would be left grieving at Ardshee if the Prince was defeated. Perhaps she was just tired, drained of any emotion but the longing for home. Though she did not sleep much during the night they passed at a roadside inn.

Then at last, next morning, they left the mountains

behind, and the road, wider and well-surfaced now, ran between fields which even in winter looked amazingly lush and fertile. Prosperous farmsteads, tidy towns and villages provided a poignant contrast with the untamed landscape she had grown to know so well. When they paused to rest or change horses the sound of English spoken on all sides seemed strange and unfamiliar, clipped, orderly, as brisk and prosperous as the landscape.

And then, towards evening, she began to see sights she knew, the shape of a hill, a farm house, the name on a milestone. They were familiar, loved and yet clothed in strangeness, as if remembered from a dream. By the time they reached the edge of her home town, and turned into the street where she had lived for so many years, Isobel realised that everything had changed.

Not that in any sense the houses were different from the ones she had left that summer Sunday. Not that the people in the street looked like any but the neighbours she had known all her life. But she knew as John helped her from the coach and her mother came running from the house to greet her, that she herself had changed beyond recognition. Nothing could ever be the same as it had once been.

Weeping and laughing together her mother clasped her in her arms, exclaiming at her odd clothes, at the dreadful fears they had felt for her, and their joy at having her home again. Her father hovered beside her, waiting to embrace her in his turn.

Then they were in the house, and her mother was asking what she wished to do first. Would she like to take some tea, or change out of those dreadful clothes?

She sipped the tea, feeling out of place in the pretty parlour, aware of the peat smoke scenting her hair, the primitive plaid contrasting with the civilised decencies of her parents' way of life. It was a relief to escape upstairs, to the room which she had so often dreamed of, and which seemed in some way shrunken and unfamiliar.

She washed in warm scented water and dressed in a

neat grey silk gown, and tidied her hair away under a little frilled cap. She could scarcely breathe for the constricting whalebones of the bodice, laced tightly across her, and the buckled shoes were harsh to her feet after the soft deerskin she had discarded. She had felt out of place before: now she felt stiff and awkward and uncomfortable.

The same constraint silenced her when John had taken his leave, promising to call again in the morning, and she was alone at last with her parents. She had longed for this moment, prayed for it desperately ever since Hector had snatched her away, and now it was as if it had all gone wrong.

There was so much to tell them, so much they wanted to know, yet she did not know where to begin. Nor was she sure that she could ever make them understand even a little of all that had happened to her. Here, with her beloved parents, she felt suddenly more lonely, more isolated than she had during the long months at Ardshee.

Tears filled her eyes as she sat at the fireside, hands clasped tightly in her lap. She answered her parents' questions in subdued monosyllables, aware of their puzzled concern.

'What is the matter with me?' she thought desperately.

'You must be very tired,' said her mother at last, after a longer silence than usual. 'When you have slept you will feel better, and then we can talk.'

She steered Isobel gently upstairs again, and helped her to undress. And then she tucked her daughter into bed, murmuring soothingly:

'You are home now, my lamb. Home and safe, and no one shall ever take you from us again.'

Later, when Isobel lay alone in the dark, she thought of her mother's words. And it struck her, chillingly, that she had already been taken from home and that the enforced parting had in a way been final and irrevocable. This orderly house was no longer home to her, and never would be again. Her parents's love was real, but it could not reach her. The dream she had cherished was an illusion.

She turned on her side and closed her eyes and the misery which should have ended with her homecoming lay cold and heavy on her heart.

CHAPTER
TEN

WHEN Isobel woke next morning she felt a little more cheerful. She climbed out of bed, threw a wrap about her shoulders and crossed to the window. It was a crisp sunny morning, the air bright with the distinctive clarity of the eastern sky, quite unlike the soft misty light of the west which she had known at Ardshee.

It was only to be expected, she thought, that it would take her a little time to grow used to being at home. She had been away for a long time, and such a great deal had happened to her meanwhile. The strangeness would pass after a day or two.

She dressed and went down to the sunlit parlour to breakfast. Her parents were as attentive as ever, hovering solicitously over her, urging her to eat, watching every mouthful for signs that her appetite was not all it should be, and her face for traces of sleeplessness or unhappiness.

At last she could bear it no longer. She put down her cup and raised her eyes to their anxious faces, and said:

'Don't watch me all the time like that! You must believe that I am well, and very soon, I expect, I shall grow used to being at home, but,' she bent her head abruptly, as the tears filled her eyes, 'but just now I . . . I . . .' And then, not knowing what she would have said and overcome by an uncontrollable flood of tears she ran from the room and threw herself on her bed.

Much later, red-eyed but composed again, Isobel joined her mother by the fire in the best parlour, bringing some long-neglected needlework to occupy her hands while she sat. Margaret Reid looked up as her daughter came in, but said nothing, waiting patiently for Isobel herself to speak when she chose. They sewed vigorously, needles flashing in the sunlight, the embroidered patterns on their work steadily growing. The soft crackle and hiss of the burning logs, the occasional sound of a passing carriage or hurrying feet outside, only emphasised the silence.

In the end Margaret could bear it no longer.

'It is nearly eleven,' she said, glancing at the ornate clock on the mantelpiece. 'John Campbell said he would call this morning.'

'Yes,' said Isobel, without discernible emotion.

Margaret's hands fell to her lap and lay still.

'Isobel,' she began gently, 'you have suffered greatly. But the nightmare is over now. Very soon you will realise that. We shall take every step in our power to help you to put it all behind you, as if it had never been. I am only sorry that you have been forced to . . .' her eyes travelled briefly to Isobel's stomach ' . . . to carry the consequences. It is so unjust! But we can try to make even that easier for you. You must bear the child, of course: that is unavoidable. But once it is born we can send it away. There are plenty of poor women glad to give their services to unwanted infants, for a fee. Then it will be as if you had never met that dreadful man.'

Isobel raised her head, her eyes on her mother's face, full of distress.

'No!' she exclaimed, with a force which took her mother—and herself—by surprise. 'No, mother. I don't want that. I want this baby, I want to hold him in my arms and care for him and love him as long as he needs me.'

Margaret listened in amazement.

'But, Isobel, you will not be able to look on the child without remembering how it came to be conceived. And what if it should resemble its father?'

Isobel had a sudden clear mental picture of herself lying in bed looking down at the tiny defenceless creature cradled in her arms, seeing Hector's dark eyes gazing up at her from beneath long lashes and the soft fuzz of dark curls covering the little head, feeling the small fingers, long for one so small, clutching at her own.

Her heart lurched, and then settled into a quickened beat. She came back to the present, to her hands at rest on her sewing, her empty lap, and was swept with longing for the moment when the child growing within her should be a reality at last.

She looked up.

'I want this baby,' she said stubbornly.

Her mother sighed, close to exasperation.

'I don't understand you, Isobel,' she said.

Nor do I, reflected Isobel, slowly resuming her sewing. For her mother's plan made sense. She wanted desperately to put the past behind her, to start again as if it had never been. She had wanted that from the moment Hector seized her in the wood. But with Hector's child in her arms she would never be able to forget. Particularly not if, as her imagination just now had suggested, the child were to resemble him. Yet some wayward part of herself, against all reason, wanted to see that likeness in the newborn child. She found it inexplicable, beyond understanding. How then could she ever expect her mother to understand?

She shrugged hopelessly, and sewed doggedly on.

It was John Campbell's arrival which broke the lengthening silence.

'I am glad to see you looking more rested,' he said, bowing over Isobel's hand. Secretly he thought she looked as harrassed and exhausted as she had done last night. Yet she should have been more at peace now than when he had come on her at Ardshee.

He greeted Margaret with his accustomed courtesy, and she rang for refreshment as he took his seat between them.

Isobel watched him while his attention was on her mother. He sat at his ease, knowing he was welcome and among friends, yet even in relaxation his body was a little awkward, ungraceful. She could not imagine him dancing in the firelight to the music of the pipes. She even smiled a little at the thought, and he turned his head at that moment and caught her expression.

'I am glad to see that smile!' he said warmly. 'That is

more like the old Isobel—Mrs Carnegie—I mean—' his
words tailed off in confusion.

'Mrs MacLean,' she corrected him steadily, and was
astonished to detect a note almost of pride in her voice.
So Hector himself might have spoken, full of his sense of
family honour.

Perhaps, she thought, I am rather enjoying all this
concern on my behalf. Perhaps I am quite glad to have
achieved such notoriety, to have gone through all these
adventures, far removed from the experience of most
girls of my age. But she sensed that this was not the
whole explanation, nor even possibly a part of it. There
was something there which she did not want to recognise
or to accept at present. She turned her attention to
Janet, coming in just then with a tray of madeira and
almond biscuits.

But John was not so readily distracted. He waited
until Janet had gone again, clearly impatient to speak,
and then burst out:

'We shall rid you of that name, my dear. You can be
Mrs Carnegie again, as if all this had never happened.'

That phrase again. But Isobel said nothing, only
giving John her full attention, grave and silent.

'You see,' he explained, leaning forward, his hands on
his knees, 'by law your marriage was no marriage, and
may be set aside—'

'But I am with child,' protested Isobel.

'Ah!' John raised his hand in reassurance. Clearly the
lawyer in him was enjoying the situation. 'But that is
beside the point. If the marriage was forced upon you
against your will, and consummated by an act of rape,
then it is no marriage. Consent is the essential factor in
the legality of any bond entered into by man and woman.
But in your case there was clearly no consent. It was a
brutal act forced upon you with violence by a man who
wanted only—one assumes—to acquire your considerable fortune. To set that marriage aside, even after
several months, will, in your case, be little more than a
formality.'

Isobel gazed down at her hands, indefinably depressed by the cool analysis of her situation, the dry lawyer's language. Then a new aspect of her predicament struck her.

'But that would make my baby a bastard!' she protested. 'Wouldn't it?'

Before John could reply her mother gently intervened.

'You see, my dear, that is why it would be better for the child to be sent away. Better for everyone.'

Isobel stared at her. Better for her parents, she acknowledged, for they would not then have to face the shame of having a bastard raised under their roof. For herself, too, it might arguably be better, in spite of what she felt, for she would be able to start a new life. But for the child—even with her limited experience of such matters she knew that to put a child out to nurse as her mother had suggested was often a tidy, discreet way of conniving at its death. Unwanted babies born to erring but respectable mothers were often despatched to wet-nurses in the full knowledge that half-hearted care, neglect even, would generally quickly rid them of the embarrassment. Better far, Isobel thought, that her baby should have the care of a woman such as Mairi MacLean, honoured to be trusted with the upbringing of a son of her chieftain.

She shook her head with renewed vehemence.

'No,' she said. 'You will not send my child away. I am his mother, and his place is with me.'

John reached out and took her hand in his.

'Isobel,' he implored earnestly, 'your feelings do you credit. You have a good, kind heart, and it is natural that you should want to do the best for your unborn child, however unhappy may have been the circumstances of its conception. But think, I beg of you, if it would indeed be the best, even for the infant, to rear it as your own among your own people. Remember who the father was—though I know it must pain you to have that brought to mind—remember what blood it is that will run in your infant's veins. The child comes of tainted stock, Isobel. Do you indeed want to rear the latest in a line of lying, murderous cattle thieves? For blood will out, my dear, believe me. Do what you will, the evil strain is there. You know a little of what my own line has suffered at the hands of a MacLean of Ardshee. But we are not alone: there have been many before and since who have cursed the fate which caused their path to cross with some scion of that evil house. No, the truly kind course is to harden your heart and let the line end with you. Root out the evil, destroy it, let the name of MacLean be lost to Ardshee, as dust in the wind.'

The light blue eyes gleamed with a cold light which sent a shiver down Isobel's spine. John was suddenly a stranger, no longer the kindly friend who had counselled and supported her through many anxieties and troubles. She recoiled, drawing her hand from his, repelled that he should so callously urge her to murder her child. For that, she knew, was what his words implied.

Even her mother evidently thought he had gone too far, for Isobel saw her touch his arm, murmuring 'John—' as if in gentle protest.

'Do you not think my blood is more than a match for any MacLean infusion?' Isobel demanded indignantly.

All at once John looked confused, his colour rising a little.

'Of course, but—' He waved a hand dismissively. 'No matter. There will be time enough for us to decide what to do before the child is born. For now you need only concern yourself with the annulment of your marriage. It should not require a great deal on your part: a brief court appearance, at the most, and no judge would look on you with anything but the deepest sympathy. Then, the formalities over, you may call yourself Isobel Carnegie again and you will be free. And able, of course—' he paused, recollecting himself, and then went on smoothly: 'But that can wait. The wheels are already set in motion. It should not take long—'

Isobel felt dazed and bewildered. She felt as if she were being pushed inexorably into some course of action she did not want to follow. Yet it was, surely, what she wished above all?

'I need time,' she faltered. 'Let me have time to think.'

'To think of what?' John asked in surprise. 'There is no difficulty that I can see. A slight formality, as I said—'

'I don't know . . .' she returned hesitantly. Her mother broke in.

'I think Isobel is still very tired. She is not herself. Come and talk it over again tomorrow, John, when she has had a little longer to rest. I think that would be better.'

With obvious reluctance, John abandoned the subject and began to talk of the weather. Isobel relapsed into a relieved silence, and let the talk circulate about her confused brain, taking in nothing that was said. For the first time in her life she was thankful when John took his leave of them.

She felt inexpressibly weary by the end of the morning, as if the effort of talking and listening and explaining had all been too much for her. She ate little at midday, and was grateful when her mother suggested she should rest.

'In your condition,' observed Margaret Reid, 'you cannot expect to be as active as you once were.'

Isobel remembered how she had walked at Ardshee, and how confinement had chafed her. She had been energetic enough there. But of course there had been the long journey since then, and the excitement, and the many demands on her emotions. She allowed her mother to tuck her into bed and pull the curtains around her and leave her alone with her thoughts.

One thing only was clear, as it had been since her mother had first broached the subject. She wanted this child. No one, she determined, should ever succeed in shaking her resolution to cherish and love him as if his conception had been entirely normal and happy.

But of course, she realised suddenly, his conception had indeed been happy. Eyes closed, she brought that last night with Hector to mind. Until now she had only remembered its ending, his calculating demands on her, his anger, his vindictiveness in making her a close prisoner.

Now she thought of the moment when he had come home, and a new warmth had seemed to spring up between them. It had been a delusion, she knew that now, for he had acted the part of the ardent lover to win her to his will. But that did not make her own feelings the less real because he had so coldly used them.

No, she had been happy then, for those few sweet hours. Happy as she had not thought it was possible to be, completely, ecstatically happy. This unborn child within her had been conceived in joy, at the moment when her whole world had been suffused in a golden light. It was, she thought now, as if for that little while she had been whole and complete as never before nor since. In Hector's approval, in his seeming warmth, in his arms, she had, fleetingly, found her home.

That then, she understood, as her heart beat faster, was why Hector's deceit, and his anger, had hurt her so much. That was why her pleasure in being at Ardshee had been so shattered by his going. That, above all, was why this place where she now lay could never be home to her again.

Everything fell into place, neatly, inexorably. She loved Hector: whatever he had done, whatever he was, she loved him. And without him, whether at Ardshee or in the parlour downstairs, she was lost and alone, for in his arms that one night she had found her heart's desire.

She knew, too, with relentless clarity, that until she could win her way back to that lost paradise she would never truly be happy again. It was an impossible dream, but it was her only hope.

And then she remembered the child—Hector's child—growing within her, and she felt a leap of joy. For surely, surely, Hector must come to care for her, once he knew! Surely he must learn to love the woman who was to bear his child. Somehow she must go to him, and tell him the news, and let him see her pride and happiness in it.

For that, she knew, she would need all her strength.

Stubbornly, full of new determination, she set herself to empty her mind of all thought, and to relax, and so drift slowly into healing sleep.

CHAPTER
ELEVEN

ISOBEL had to admit next morning that all was not well. Despite the long hours of rest she felt draggingly tired, and her back and limbs ached unbearably. She would very much have liked to stay in bed all day. But she had no intention of allowing her parents to know how she felt. Full of determination she dressed and went down-stairs and dismissed any comments on her grey face and general air of exhaustion. She knew that today, as soon as possible, she must make them all understand what she meant to do.

Her determination was not strong enough for her to broach the subject before John came, earlier than usual, to talk to her. And she found herself alone with him at the parlour fireside almost before she had time to collect her thoughts.

He stood leaning one arm against the mantelpiece, waiting for her to sit down before he began. But she remained standing, ignoring her weary protesting body, and drew a deep breath.

'Mr Campbell,' she said quietly, but with such a note of deep gravity that she had his full attention at once. 'I think I should say first of all that I do not wish to have my marriage to Hector MacLean set aside.'

She waited for his outburst, but her words were met with a blank stare, as if their meaning must lie hidden beneath the apparent clarity of what she said. After a moment he sighed, rather as if he were a long-suffering adult faced with a much-loved but particularly trying child, and then he took her arm.

'Sit down, my dear, and let us talk about this calmly. You look as if you were expecting to face a firing party.' He smiled gently, and she allowed him to lead her to a chair and to take his seat facing her, holding her hands in his. 'Now, my dear,' he went on, still in that kindly tone, 'tell me what troubles you about our proposal. It is the child, I suppose? You cannot bear to have your infant made a bastard?'

'No,' said Isobel. 'It's not that.'

John frowned, genuinely puzzled.

'But what then? What other possible objection can you have? I suppose, of course, that you have some firm objection, and that this is not just a sudden whim due to your present delicate condition?'

She looked down at his hands as they held hers: long hands, pale and a little puffy, the hands of a man who passed much of his time indoors and worked with his brain. Not like those other hands, lean and strong and brown . . .

She realised that John was still waiting for her answer, and coloured, trying to remember what she had meant to say.

'I . . . I . . . no . . .' She broke off, and began again with renewed firmness. 'No, it is not a whim, Mr Campbell. And it is not just the child, though I think that must be a part of it. But even if I were not in this condition I should still feel the same way, I am sure of that.' She raised her eyes to his and caught their expression of patient and affectionate bewilderment, and found that she could not go on as she had intended. 'Just believe, please, that I have my own reasons for not wanting to take my marriage before the courts. It can make little difference, after all.'

She hoped he would believe that, for she knew that it was not true. She at least hoped that it would make all the difference, that she might soon return to Hector. But John Campbell must surely expect her to remain at home now, living quietly with her parents to the end of her days.

She was not prepared for the vehemence of his reaction. His hands tightened about hers, and his eyes held hers with a light she had never seen in them before.

'It makes all the difference in the world,' he retorted

fiercely. 'For you will be tied as long as Ardsheé lives, his wife in law—'

'But surely I am already ruined in the eyes of the world?' she argued. 'No man would want me after all that has happened.'

Even as she spoke she knew with an inexplicable sinking of the heart what John's reply would be. And it came, spoken in a low voice vibrant with intense feelings rigorously held down.

'You are wrong, Isobel, wholly wrong. For I had hoped—longed—Isobel, whatever you choose you will be alone but for your parents, with no husband to stand beside you through the years to come. But if you were once free, your marriage set aside, then, Isobel—then nothing would make me happier than to offer you the protection of my hand and my name.'

'You do me great honour,' she said gravely, 'but I am not seeking the protection of any man.'

'It is not simply my protection I offer, Isobel,' John went on. 'It is my heart too. You know, I think, that I have always cared for you—'

Her eyes now were warm with affection, and pity, because she knew that she must tell him everything, and that it would hurt him.

'John, don't say any more: just listen to me. I am greatly honoured that you should make me such an offer, and as your friend I thank you from the bottom of my heart. But I cannot accept your hand, though I hope I shall always have your friendship. Once . . . before . . . soon after James died . . . Then, if you had asked, I might have said yes. In fact I think I would have done so. Because, you see, I had never known then what it is to love. When you don't know what you are missing, then I think you are quite happy to think that friendship is enough. But now I do know what I missed then—'

'So there is another man!' he exclaimed. 'But who—where—?' Clearly, to John Campbell, the truth was going to be beyond belief.

'I am married to him,' Isobel told him quietly. 'I bear his name.'

For a moment he gazed at her blankly, outright disbelief giving way slowly to a growing horror.

'Ardshee?' he whispered incredulously. 'You love *him* . . . Hector MacLean?' She said nothing, steadily returning his gaze, and he burst out: 'No! I will not believe it. You're playing with me, Isobel—I don't know why, but that must be it—'

'I am not playing,' she told him. 'I was never more serious in my life.' To emphasise her point, she went on: 'I know you find it hard to understand, but it is true. I love Hector MacLean.' She spoke proudly, with a lift of the head, and then repeated: 'I love him, and I will never love anyone else as long as I live. And I am proud to be his wife.'

The declaration almost startled her in its forcefulness. That it was devastating to John was even more apparent. He rose to his feet and stood behind his chair, gripping the brocaded back as if he had Hector's neck beneath his hands.

'You are deluded! You must be! Isobel, you know what he is—I told you—you cannot be so blind. Surely you do not think he cares for you? He wants your money, that's all. Why else would he carry you off in that fashion? A loving man would have wooed you openly, with honour. But he carried you off as he would raid a neighbour's cattle, for his own gain and the love of villainy. How can you be such a fool?'

She smiled wryly.

'I don't know,' she admitted. 'But I am.'

'Have you any reason to think he cares for you?' John asked sharply.

Isobel thought of that last night with Hector, and how it had ended, and then slowly shook her head.

'No,' she said. 'No reason at all.'

John crashed his fist down on the back of the chair.

'Then why be such a fool? Oh, he has some kind of wild charm, I suppose, at least for a young girl innocent of the world and its ways—but he is evil, Isobel, utterly evil, believe me. You would never, ever find happiness with him, even if he came to care for you. And you know yourself that he will not. To give your heart to him is like giving your soul to the devil—you will be lost—'

'No, John,' she corrected him quietly. 'I am lost without him.'

'Then you must be saved from yourself!' he asserted with decision. 'It is your parents' wish, as well as mine, that you should be freed of all connection with this man. He must have no possible hope of ever laying hands upon your fortune. It would have been better if you could have appeared in court to put your case, but it can be done without you if necessary.'

'What do you mean?' she asked, alarmed.

'Here—' He thrust his hand inside his coat and drew out an untidy sheaf of papers from an inner pocket. She came to his side and waited as he sifted through them, letting one fall unnoticed to the ground. Then with a grunt of satisfaction he drew out a folded paper in what she saw at once was her own handwriting.

'There!' he said, smiling triumphantly. 'All the proof the court needs that you were forced into marriage against your will and at no time consented to what happened to you. A letter sent by you to your parents while you were Ardshee's prisoner.'

Isobel turned white.

'But . . . but I wrote no such letter! I could not have done . . .'

'But the court will not know that,' John assured her. He was calm now, with a quiet smiling air of confidence which had something oddly menacing about it. 'You must admit the handwriting is most convincing.' She stared at him, slowly realising what he implied: that he, the respectable lawyer, had stooped to forgery.

'You surely cannot mean to do this, John,' she whispered. 'You know how I feel. Let me have that letter—or throw it on the fire. Accept that if I am lost to you as a wife I am nevertheless still your devoted—and grateful—friend.'

He thrust the letter quickly back inside his coat.

'No!' he exclaimed harshly. 'No, Isobel Carnegie, you shall not remain my friend. I do not want your friendship—have never wanted it. And I shall have you, somehow, whatever the cost—'

'You would not force me to marry you?' she asked incredulously. 'But that's just what you condemn Hector for!'

He turned then and grasped her arms, so fiercely that it hurt.

'If that damned thieving savage had not come along when he did, you would have had me. You said it yourself just now. If I had Ardshee in my hands at this moment as I have you I would break him in little pieces and scatter his carcase to the four winds and rejoice to think that I had sent his black soul to roast in Hell where it belongs. And I should number the torments he suffered one by one and set them against the wrong he has done me, against my father's murder and his taking of you—'

'But you said it was his father killed your father,' she protested, her sense of justice breaking through her mounting horror at this terrible outpouring.

'It is all one,' he went on, and the cold gleam in his eyes grew, becoming more chilling with every angry word. 'The same tainted blood runs in them all. He shall not have you, Isobel. You are mine, and I shall fight to make that true in law as it is in nature.'

'You cannot want me to be wed to you against my will!' Isobel felt as if her cry rose and beat against his anger and hate as ineffectually as the waves beat on the rocks at Ardshee.

'I don't give a damn what you want,' returned John. 'I shall have you—somehow I shall have you. And if I can't have you through the courts then I shall seek out Hector MacLean and make you a widow again and free you that way. Make no mistake, Isobel, there is no escape.'

What he would have said or done then, Isobel was not to know, though she could not imagine there was any more to be said. But at that moment her mother came in, quiet and courteous and smiling, and looking all at once quite out of place in that atmosphere seething with hate and anger.

'Well, is it all sorted out?' she asked cheerfully, and

then paused, sensing from the way John and Isobel had sprung apart that she had interrupted something not meant for her ears. Looking from one grim face to the other she was not reassured.

'What's wrong? Have you two been quarrelling? Isobel, you do not look at all well this morning—John, bring some wine if you please.'

Isobel sank down on the nearest chair, feeling all at once limp and exhausted. It was as if her normal everyday world had turned suddenly to nightmare. She could not yet grasp all the implications of what had passed between them.

She sipped the wine when it came and felt a little better, and leaned back in the chair with eyes closed as her mother questioned John.

'I think we can see the matter through the courts without bringing her into it,' John was saying smoothly. 'It would be rather too much for her, I think, after all she has been through—and in her condition—'

The kindly, considerate friend! Isobel heard her mother murmuring her agreement, and then they moved off towards the window so as not to disturb her with their talking. She moved restlessly in the chair, trying to find a more comfortable position. Her back ached abominably.

Her slippered foot brushed against something close to the chair, and she opened her eyes to see what it was. She remembered the paper which had fallen as John searched for the letter. It lay there still, forgotten. Idly she picked it up and looked at it, straining to hear what they were saying. It was a moment or two before her brain registered the words which her eyes read.

Whoever had written this note—and she could not decipher the signature—was demanding the return of five thousand pounds from John Campbell, and threatening a court action and the inevitable exposure which this would involve. It had been written within the past week, but clearly the money had been owing for very much longer than that.

She let her hands fall to her lap, trapping the paper

beneath them. She felt cold, but detached and very clear-headed. Many things were falling relentlessly into place.

John Campbell had been her friend for three years now. He had come into her life while she was married to James Carnegie and yet daily expecting his death. He had known, of course, as James's man of business, that she would be likely to inherit a vast fortune on her husband's death. And it was possible, judging by the tone of this letter, that even then he had been in some kind of financial difficulty.

She had found it strange and alarming just now to hear John talk of forcing her to repudiate Hector and marry him. John, the kind friend, who should, whatever his own feelings, have understood what she felt, and respected her wish to remain Hector's wife.

But if John Campbell had hoped to marry her for her fortune, and found himself thwarted by Hector's more direct manner of achieving the same end. If he had then rescued Isobel, expecting to use his legal skills to free her, and then found that she did not, after all, want to be freed to marry her old friend. If all that were true, then it made some kind of dreadful sense of this morning's scene.

She looked round at the two figures at the window, deep in earnest conversation.

'Mother,' she called. 'I should like to speak to John alone. Please would you leave us for a moment?'

A little surprised, but happy enough to comply, her mother left them alone together. John crossed the room to stand beside her, all smiling calmness again.

'Have you thought better of it then, my dear?' he asked amiably.

'No,' she replied. 'I have found this. You dropped it.' And she handed him the paper.

She watched him turn white and then red, and then fold the paper with trembling fingers.

'Just a trifle,' he said casually, though she caught the anxiety in his tone as he replaced the paper inside his coat.

'I don't think it is,' she contradicted him. 'I think in fact that it explains a great deal.'

'I don't know what you mean,' he returned coldly.

'But I think you do. If I am wrong, then I suppose no apology on my part could make up for what I am thinking now. But I am afraid I am not wrong. It explains so much.'

His hand closed about her wrist, gently and yet with a pressure behind it in which she detected a threat.

'You are not well, Isobel. You ought to go and rest. You will see when you feel better that you have entertained unjust suspicions of me. I am your friend, Isobel, and always have been.'

'And if I had been little Isobel Reid, with only a modest portion to my name, what then?'

'I am your friend,' he repeated doggedly, but she read the answer in his eyes.

She stood up, fired with sudden anger.

'How dare you, John Campbell! How dare you speak ill of anyone for seeking to do what you have plotted and deceived and connived to achieve for years and years and years. You insinuated yourself into James Carnegie's house, and into my affections, with one aim only, one base, despicable aim, to step into James's shoes when the poor man should die. I am glad Hector MacLean thwarted you, John, glad he took me out of your clutches! And you can be quite sure that there will be no second chance. If you take this matter to court then I shall demand to appear and I shall swear on oath that I chose to go with Hector, that I loved him from the first moment I saw him, that I am proud to be his wife and to bear his child and his name. And if that's perjury then I don't care because in its own way it is all completely true. And as for you, I never want to see you again as long as I live—'

She saw John gazing at her open-mouthed, astonished at her outburst, and as she finished the cold threatening gleam lit his eyes again and she braced herself to face the inevitable anger. And then all at once she could not see him clearly, for a mist seemed to have descended between them. Her head throbbed clamorously.

She saw him spring towards her, felt his fingers on her throat, and knew she was falling. She clutched out wildly for some support and a great pain shot through her body, driving out every other thought and feeling.

A long way off someone screamed, horribly, and she did not know that it was herself.

CHAPTER
TWELVE

SLOWLY Isobel opened her eyes.

The room was quiet and dark, lit only by the leaping flames of the fire whose gentle crackling reached her through the stillness. She felt strange: very tired, insubstantial, remote. It was some time before she remembered where she was.

She moved her head, just a little, towards the firelight. It took all her strength to complete the tiny manoeuvre. And it brought Janet into view, sitting at the bedside gazing at her with an expression on her face such as Isobel had never seen there before. Why, thought Isobel, should the maid have that look of anxious love? Why, next, did she slide onto her knees by the bed and take Isobel's hand in hers and stroke her hair, with tears pouring unchecked down her face? Isobel tried to ask why, but she could not find the strength to frame the words.

As Janet poured out her relief and thankfulness, Isobel tried to remember how she had come to be here. But she could bring to mind only a confused recollection of nightmare and pain, grotesque faces bending over her and receding, voices whose quietest tones reverberated through an aching head; and always a dreadful tearing pain.

She felt Janet lift her head and hold a cup to her lips, and drank from it thankfully. And then she slid back into the deep untroubled sleep from which she had awakened just now.

When she woke again it was daylight, and no one sat between the bed and the fire, though some needlework lay abandoned on the bedside chair. She felt unbelievably weak still, but her mind was clearer, and that overwhelming weariness had left her. She even felt a little hungry.

She lay enjoying the peace of the room, the comfort of the clean smooth sheet beneath her. Someone must have changed the bedding, she thought, for it had not always been like that. Piece by piece the past came back to her.

She had been very ill, that much was clear. Before that, long before, she had met Hector in the garden. The little scene stood out clearly in her memory, his lithe figure vividly alive under the orchard trees. Those dark eyes had haunted her illness. She had seemed to see him always a long way off, and she could never make him hear her, cry out as she would.

Her husband. Hector MacLean who had carried her to Ardshee, and whom she loved. She closed her eyes and smiled gently to herself. She was to bear his child and perhaps, when he knew, he would love her for it. She laid her hands over the place where the child was growing. Her body was painfully thin, her stomach flat as a girl's.

Panic rising in her, she remembered the rest. John, the friend turned suddenly to a terrible enemy. The quarrel, some dreadful moment of danger which she could not clearly bring to mind. And then the illness—

She gave a cry of anguish and her mother, who had wandered for a moment to the window, came swiftly to her side.

'My wee lamb,' she crooned, drawing Isobel into her arms. 'Wisht now, my love. It is all over.'

Her face muffled against her mother's soft shoulder, Isobel struggled to speak.

'The baby . . . mother, the baby . . .!'

Her mother kissed her and laid her gently back against the pillow, smoothing her hair.

'Just get well now, my darling. Don't fret about anything.'

Isobel felt tears flood her eyes. Could her mother not understand what she was asking?

'Mother,' she whispered through dry lips, 'will the baby be all right?'

Her mother sat down heavily on the edge of the bed and took one thin hand in hers, stroking it tenderly.

'I am sorry, Isobel. You have lost the baby. But do not grieve. It will be for the best, you will see.'

But Isobel was not listening. She lay heaving with silent sobs, the tears trickling from her closed lids over her sunken cheeks and onto the pillow. The last lingering hope had gone from her world, and she was desolate.

It was a long time before at last the tears subsided and she lay exhausted, longing for the release of sleep, closing her eyes against the anxious faces hovering over her. She resisted their coaxing attempts to make her eat and drink, for why should she do as they said and build up her strength? There was nothing to live for now. Their despair left her unmoved, for hers was greater.

The physician came and clucked over her and prescribed this medicine and that. Her mother wept and her father pleaded, but still she lay there, listless and apathetic, unwilling to make the effort they asked of her.

Late one evening she woke from a brief restless sleep to find Janet once more at her bedside. That in itself was a relief, for Janet did not, after that first moment, weep and plead and trouble her with incessant demands to do this or try that. Instead she sat quietly, and smiled as Isobel's eyes reached her face. And when she spoke, there was no mention of Isobel herself.

'The snowdrops are out in the garden,' she said quietly.

Isobel felt her mouth tremble and the tears fill her eyes, but she swallowed hard.

'Oh,' was all she could say, in a harsh whisper.

'It will soon be spring,' Janet went on, in the same cheerfully conversational tone. 'Though it's been a hard winter this year.'

Isobel thought fleetingly of the women at Ardshee singing through cracked lips as they laboured in the biting wind. A hard winter would leave them close to starvation. It would have been good to take her wealth with her to bring them food, and sound roofs over their heads . . .

She raised her eyes to the maid's broad rosy face.

'Janet,' she said, 'shall I tell you something?'

'You can tell me whatever you like,' answered Janet, her voice still robustly non-committal.

'I should like to go back to Ardshee,' Isobel told her, watching Janet's face for any sign of astonishment or disapproval. But Janet simply nodded.

'I thought you might,' she commented. 'You were calling out enough when you were ill. You get well, my lass, and then you can go back, if that's what you want.'

Without further ado she went to the fireside and brought a bowl of broth to Isobel, helping her to sip it a little at a time.

Afterwards, trying hard to conceal her delight, she returned the empty bowl to its place, and laid her hand over Isobel's, saying very gently: 'You love that man, my lass, don't you?'

'Yes,' admitted Isobel. And she poured all her fears and hopes and griefs into Janet's sympathetic but unde-manding ears.

Her parents were jubilant at Isobel's first hesitant step on the road to recovery. But they were too afraid of a relapse to make their delight too obvious. Awed by Janet's success, they were careful to follow her advice in their manner towards their daughter. There were no more over-anxious requests for her to eat or drink, and all possible sensitive topics of conversation were strenu-ously avoided.

It was Isobel herself who had to ask directly for news, for as she grew stronger there were many things she wanted to know.

'Has Mr Campbell called at all since I became ill?' Isobel asked as she sat up in bed one afternoon, idly turning the pages of a book.

Margaret Reid looked up from her sewing, frowning slightly.

'No, he hasn't,' she admitted. 'I find that a little strange. He was most distressed when you were taken ill so suddenly. He was kindness itself, too, and ran for the doctor and did all he could. We fully expected that he would call many times to ask how you did. But we have not seen him since. And,' she went on, rather more hesitantly, 'I don't know that I should speak of it, but they say he has left town. To raise a troop for the King, some say. Though I have also heard talk of money troubles—but you know how people will gossip, and I find that hard to believe. It is strange, though, when he was such a close friend. You would have thought—' She smiled suddenly. 'But there now, perhaps he'll come back soon.'

Isobel thought it most unlikely, but said nothing. Clearly her parents had no suspicion as to what had passed between the two of them that day.

'He was always a good loyal King's man,' Margaret went on. 'I think it very possible he felt his duty called him to take up arms against the rebels.'

The rebels. Isobel felt a twinge of alarm. She had heard no news since she and John had talked together on the way back from Ardshee. The Prince's army had been in England then. With a beating heart she questioned her mother.

'Will they succeed, do you think?' she asked, not quite knowing what answer she hoped for. So long as Hector was safe—

'To be open with you, Isobel, no one seems very sure what will happen,' her mother explained. 'When the rebels retreated from England we all thought it only a matter of time—and then they took Stirling, and won another victory, at Falkirk this time, and they still hold much of Scotland. Though we thank God daily that they have passed us by here. We have all had endless sleepless nights fearing what might happen. However, we hear that their supplies are low, and in this cold weather—' She shrugged eloquently. 'We shall have to see. It is hard to believe that a handful of ragged Highlanders can hold out much longer against the best modern troops—yet we hear that they are irresistible in the heat of battle. On each occasion it has been our men who have fled from the field in terror, though we have the guns and the muskets and they have only swords and shields for the most part. Still, the King has sent the Duke of Cumberland to take charge now, and for all his youth he is said to be a fine general. No, surely in the end the King must have the victory.'

And whether they met with victory or defeat, Hector must soon go home to Ardshee. And she would not be there to welcome him.

'Mother,' she decided with sudden vigour, 'as soon as I am well I shall go back to Ardshee.'

Margaret was white-faced and motionless with shock, her needle suspended in mid-air.

'Isobel! You can't be serious! You were to end your marriage—though you did talk of that man in your fever . . .'

'I shall remain his wife, and I shall go back to Ardshee,' said Isobel firmly.

Her mother was silent, clearly searching frantically for the right words to use in this suddenly perilous situation.

'Don't be hasty, Isobel,' she advised at last, trying to sound like any reasonable mother counselling her daughter on a trivial matter. 'I think it would be sensible to wait until the outcome of the rebellion is clear, and you know what has become of your husband. If they are defeated, he may well find his property is forfeited, and you as his wife would lose all your fortune too. If you remain here they will leave you alone, knowing you had no part in it.' She saw that Isobel was unmoved by this argument, except possibly to a greater sympathy towards Hector. She went on hastily: 'In any case, the country is so troubled that it would be most unwise to travel so far, particularly as your health is not all it ought to be.'

'I shall wait until I'm well,' Isobel conceded, and with that her mother had to be content. It was as well she did not realise that it was not a concession at all.

Once she was determined to recover, Isobel quickly regained her strength, though it was almost the end of March before she knew that she could consider facing the long and arduous journey to Ardshee.

The prospect was a terrifying one, and would have

been so even in peace time. It was not for nothing that Hector and his men preferred to travel to and from Ardshee by sea. The deadly rocks and treacherous currents presented far less of a hazard to men familiar with their ways than the wild wastes of the mountains, the dangers to be faced from an unpredictable climate, poor roads, little shelter and the fear of robbery or murder by the wayside. And for a solitary woman, who was not even a Highlander, the journey would be hazardous in the extreme.

But Isobel acknowledged that she was utterly foolhardy even to think of attempting the journey, steadfastly put the dangers out of her mind, and set to work to make her plans.

By discreet enquiries among friends they visited as she grew fit for company again, she managed to acquire a map of sorts. She set to one side the clothes and other items she would find essential, the blue woollen dress, the plaid and the deerskin shoes—better, she thought, if she travelled in Highland dress—and some money.

March had turned to April when she was ready at last. She sat at her window in the growing dusk and tried to think how best to break the news to her parents. She had scratched out her third attempt at a letter when Janet came in, softly, without knocking.

Isobel looked up sharply, laying her hand over the untidy page. Janet quietly closed the door and came towards her.

'I know it's not my place to be told what you won't even say to your own kin,' she said, 'but that there's something going on I'm quite sure. And I can't let you run yourself into danger and pretend I know nothing of it.'

Isobel's heart beat faster, but she tried to keep her anxiety from her voice.

'How should I be running into danger?' she demanded with studied casualness.

'Well,' said Janet wisely, her head on one side, 'you might be planning to go back to that place you spoke of—Ardshee, was it now? You've been very quiet about it of late, and I don't like that. And though I've mentioned it to no one, I think it a very strange thing you should hide a map under your pillow. Did you forget I might be tidying in here one forenoon?'

Isobel reddened, chewing on the end of her quill. What could she do now? There was no point in denying it, for she could no longer hope to make her escape unseen.

'You shan't stop me,' was all she said, stubbornly.

'I didn't think I should,' returned Janet. 'But that's not to say I think you're wise. I can't see what good you'll do by going all that way.'

'I shall be at Ardshee when he returns,' Isobel reminded her. Janet's response was brutal in its frankness.

'But will he care whether you're there or not?' she asked. 'I'm sorry, my lass,' she added, seeing the stricken look in Isobel's eyes, 'but it's got to be said. You've given me no reason to think he cares for you one jot.'

'He might do,' returned Isobel bravely, 'when he sees what I have gone through to return to him. When he knows I love him.' She did not add 'when I tell him he can have every penny of my fortune', though her reason told her it was likely to be the surest way to his affections. But she knew what Janet would make of that. 'You cannot make me change my mind,' she added, for good measure.

'Then you'll not go alone,' asserted Janet. 'I'm coming with you—Now, tell me what I'll need.'

CHAPTER
THIRTEEN

THE garden was hard with frost when Isobel and Janet
stole across it just after midnight. Behind them the
house stood dark and silent, its occupants all innocently
asleep, oblivious of the shock which must await them in
the morning.

The two fugitives crept quickly through the deserted
streets of the little town and into the enveloping darkness of the countryside beyond. A small moon gave a
faint light to show them the way.

They followed the road which took them north, towards the mountains, walking in almost total silence,
anxious only to cover as much ground as possible before
dawn. Isobel knew it was more than likely that her
parents would set out in pursuit the moment they found
her gone, though she had said nothing of the route she
planned to take.

Her one hope was that they would expect her to make
for the road built some years ago by General Wade, the
only truly passable way into the Highlands for the
ordinary traveller. But that would have taken her too far
to the east, and brought her more readily into contact
with English-speaking Scots who would be able to betray
her whereabouts. And so she planned to take the north-
westerly path through glens and mountains known well
only to Highlanders. Then, if her parents did follow,
they would not easily find anyone able to speak their
language and tell them where she had gone.

When the sun rose at last they kept as far as possible to
the trees and fields close to the road, alert for
approaching traffic. At the sound of distant wheels they
would lie behind the nearest hedge, or deep in the frozen

undergrowth, until the danger had passed. It made their progress uncomfortably slow.

They reached the mountains late in the day as it began to grow dark. The lower slopes here were thickly wooded, cut with deep ravines down which the burns roared on their way to the shining waters of the many lochs, silver in the fitful moonlight. It began to snow, thin light flakes which did not settle except where the frost was at its hardest. The peaks were still white with the remnants of the last snowfall.

Once or twice Isobel hesitated, unsure of the path, and then after a moment's consideration plodded doggedly on. Slowly the tiny winding track became invisible, swallowed up in the trees and the night. Far above, stars twinkled frostily, lost now and then behind the thin cloud which brought the snow. Many times they stumbled on some hidden root or stone.

At last they came to a great moss-grown wall of rock, discernible only by a faint moonlight and their exploring hands. They could not see where the path went, but Isobel put out a hesitant foot and heard a scatter of earth and pebbles far below, where a distant rush of water told them of a fast running stream deep in the glen.

'That settles it,' Janet asserted. 'I'm not risking my neck any further. We stop right here and rest and we don't go on until we can see the path.'

With considerable reluctance Isobel had to agree. Even her longing to reach Ardshee was not proof now against her weariness. Besides, if they were to injure themselves or lose their way it could only lengthen their journey in the end. So they sank down against the rock and huddled together for warmth and managed to sleep for some hours.

At dawn they ate some of the food they carried with them and set out again. The dim grey light revealed that the path skirted the rock at a treacherous angle above the precipitous drop to the rushing waters below. Just as well, said Janet with a shudder, that they had not tried to take that way in the dark.

As the daylight grew, Isobel was forced to acknowledge that one of her fears of last night was fully justified. She no longer had any idea where they were. The endless intersecting lines of mountain and glen seemed to bear no relation to the marks on her map, and there was not even any sun in the grey sky to reassure them that they were not going in completely the wrong direction. They had no alternative but to ask for help from the first house they came upon.

They found that it was the best course they could have taken. Isobel summoned up her neglected knowledge of Gaelic, and in return they found that their journey became at once easy, comfortable, even safe. Their plight, as two women wandering lost and unprotected in the mountains, aroused all the warmth of sympathy and hospitality of the Highland people to whom a guest was sacred. They were urged to share the simple food, rest on heather beds within the dark interiors of the little houses, accept the guidance of host or hostess on the next stage of their journey. And all this without questioning or sign of suspicion.

Some days later they came at last to the ferry at Ballachulish, on the grey waters of Loch Leven, and the final stage of their journey. They were the only passengers on the boat that morning, and the ferryman maintained a sombre silence until they had reached the further shore. Then he asked casually in English if they had far to go. At Isobel's reply he shook his head.

'Ardshee, now,' he repeated gloomily. 'Would he be out following the Prince?'

It took Isobel a moment to realise that he was referring to Hector and not to his home; and then an unaccountable shiver ran down her spine.

'He is indeed,' she confirmed, and knew that she did not want to hear what the man had to say next.

'Then it will be a sad day for him, too,' continued the ferryman.

Isobel suppressed a longing to turn and walk as quickly as she could from this place. The mountains seemed suddenly oppressive, their stark shapes towering over the travellers, the water they had crossed at once dark and deep and sinister. She pulled the plaid about her in a vain attempt to keep out the chill which was creeping through her.

'Why do you say that?' she asked quietly, almost with reluctance.

'You have not heard, then?' She sensed his grim satisfaction at being first with the news. 'It would be two days ago now—a terrible day for those that were with the Prince, and an evil place, on Drummossie Moor where they met their fate. That is near Inverness, you see, and the Duke of Cumberland met them there. The Prince has fled, and his army is gone and the King of England is triumphant. There will be widows and orphans in all the Highlands now—'

Isobel stood motionless, numb fingers clenched tight on the folds of the plaid, eyes wide and dark and haunted in her white face. And then she turned to her maid with a new and desperate urgency in her voice.

'Janet, we must go on quickly. We've no time to waste. We must get to Ardshee as soon as ever we can, if we have to walk through the night.'

As they set out again, Janet said sensibly: 'I don't see why the news means we have to rush like this. I'm sure I don't want your husband to have been killed in battle, if that's what you fear, but I can't see that it helps if we hurry. In any case, why not go to Inverness and seek him there?'

'Because if he is alive, even if he is hurt, he will go to Ardshee. Can't you see that? And if the battle took place two days ago he may be there now, and in need of me.'

'I should have thought it was the last place he'd go to, as a defeated rebel,' objected Janet. 'If they're after him it's the one place they're sure to come seeking him.'

Isobel shook her head fiercely.

'No, Janet, they'd never find him at Ardshee. It's too wild and lonely a place for an army to march to. He'll be safe there—but I must be there when he comes home—' Her voice tailed off to a whisper, and Janet scarcely heard the final desolate words: 'if he comes home.'

They found a second boat to ferry them across Loch
Linnhe at the Corran narrows and then walked through
the day and most of the following night over the wild
mountains and glens of the peninsular of which Ardshee
was a part. They found their way by the sun and the
stars, for the paths and tracks were few and ill-defined.
'We must go south west,' Isobel pointed out, although
she felt sure that the force of her love was stronger than
any compass, guiding her towards home and the man she
loved.

Just after midnight Isobel halted at last and ordered a
rest.

'We must be fresh for our arrival,' she insisted. Janet
was too weary to quarrel with that argument, and they
sank down to sleep where they were.

At dawn they woke and ate their fill from the food
their last host had packed for them. There was still
barley bread and cheese enough for another meal, but
Isobel knew they would not be needing that. Even so she
resisted the temptation to feed it to the birds, just in case
anything went wrong.

But the horror of yesterday had left her now, fading in
the quiet spring morning. She was nearly home, back
where she belonged, and Hector would be there and all
would be well. She washed carefully in a nearby burn,
and combed her hair, and arranged the plaid in its most
flattering folds, joining in Janet's laughter at her efforts.

'I must look my best for my husband,' she explained
gently, her eyes bright, and Janet shook her head and
said nothing, suddenly grown serious.

It was late in the morning when they came to the
shieling ground, silent and deserted in the sunlight.
Before long, Isobel reflected, as they passed the empty
huts and climbed the hill beyond, the women and children would drive their poor cattle up here again to graze
and grow fat, and the singing and laughter would echo
around the sheltered hollow. The rebellion was over,
however unhappy its end for Hector and his people, and
life could return to its interrupted order, hard, poor, and
yet rich in love and loyalty and tradition. And Hector

would find he had a wife proud to bear his name and happy to share in his task of caring for his people. Perhaps, thought Isobel, there would soon be children, many children—

'The sea—look! And a ship, a ship in the bay!'

It was Janet's cry which broke into her happy dreams and brought Isobel instantly back to the present. A ship! Her heart gave a great leap and she gazed where Janet pointed, at the sea wide and blue below the far mountains, and a ship gently at rest at the mouth of the bay near the castle on its point. Hector was home!

And then she stood still.

The ship which lay at anchor in the water was a splendid sight, proud and magnificent, with sails furled and sunlight gleaming on polished brass and weathered timber and the sinister lines of her guns. But she bore no resemblance at all to the primitive little vessel which had carried Hector from Ardshee on that summer morning nearly a year ago. Disappointment brought a prickle of tears to Isobel's eyes, hastily brushed away.

'I think it's a naval ship,' Janet pointed out. 'They'll be busy keeping a watch on the coast, I suppose. Perhaps they want to prevent the Young Pretender from making his escape.'

They walked on towards the point where, Isobel knew, the ground fell away and they would see the castle and the bay and the settlement clearly below them. The trees on the slopes edging the bay would be misted with green and loud with birdsong, the grass laced with violets and primroses. Soon the singing of the women at their work would reach them, clear and sweet on the breeze from the sea. Eager to be with them all again, Isobel broke into a run.

She had just topped the little rise when a flock of birds flew suddenly up from the bay, clamorous with agitation, shattering the quiet of the morning. And almost at once the air was seared with a long and terrible scream of unbearable agony.

CHAPTER
FOURTEEN

JANET clutched her arm.

'Mercy on us, what was that?'

'I don't know,' whispered Isobel between white lips.

The agitated lowing of cattle reached their ears, and the crying of children. And then the sharp rattle of musket fire echoed around the cliffs.

Cold with fear Isobel took the few paces forward that brought the bay into view.

'Soldiers!' exclaimed Janet in a low voice.

Small red figures ran like ants among the clustered roofs of the settlement below. In and out of the houses, flinging cooking pots and furniture onto a great heap a short distance away; about the frightened cattle, herding them together on the ploughed strips of the clan's fields; and backwards and forwards in pursuit of wildly flapping chickens and leaping goats. And at one side the women and children stood, huddled together, ringed with red sentinels.

Alone by the door of one of the houses lay the still form of a man face down on the ground with his plaid about him, and the red of his blood bright on the grass. Even as they watched a group of soldiers dragged a second man from another house, put him roughly against a wall, and shot him. Blood reddened the white of his hair as he slid to the ground.

Isobel sank down on the grass, sickened and appalled, and met Janet's gaze full of equal horror and disbelief.

'What can we do?' mouthed the maid, as white as her mistress. 'What's happening?'

'The old men . . . they're shooting the old men who were left behind . . .' Isobel spoke as if even now she could not quite convince herself that what she had seen was real.

A third burst of musket fire rattled over the bay, and then there was a tiny, horrible pause, while the birds settled again and even the cattle were quiet. Isobel could not bring herself to look.

A scream more terrible than the first shattered the brief silence, and then was repeated, again and again and again.

On hands and knees the two watchers crept forward to where they could see. And wished at once that they had not.

It was only too clear what the soldiers were doing now, dragging the women from where they were herded like their own cattle, flinging them down on the defiled turf by their houses, raping them one after the other, while the children cried in terror and the screams rose higher and higher into the clear air.

'Mairi . . .' murmured Isobel in agony. 'Oh, dear God, what can we do?'

But she knew there was no answer, and the obscene work went on below unhindered. A child ran out from the little group towards his mother, and they saw a watching soldier strike out at him with his musket, and he fell, lying still on the grass. His mother struggled to her feet and threw herself screaming over the small body, only to be dragged aside and raped again. Isobel began to cry, with slow hard sobs which could bring no relief. She had never felt so utterly helpless as she did now.

'Your man's not there then?' Janet asked dully. It was more of a statement than a question.

'I think,' said Isobel with sudden complete conviction, 'that I would wish him dead, rather than that he should know of this.'

Yet she knew that she did not wish it for herself. She had spoken instinctively, from her love for Hector and her knowledge of what Ardshee and its people meant to him. It was that part of her now which hoped that he lay quietly on the bleak moor where his cause had met its end, past grieving for the suffering women below.

In their horrified absorption in what they saw, it had not occurred to the two watchers that there could be any danger for themselves. It was not until the gleeful shout from behind broke into their concentration that they knew that three soldiers, wandering further afield in search of other plunder, had found them.

Instinctively, aware that escape was impossible, they rose to their feet and faced the soldiers, though the naked lust in their eyes was horrible, more frightening than the levelled pistol which one of them held. The one comfort was that Janet's solidly Lowland dress made them pause for a moment, suddenly doubtful of the nature of their prey.

'You keep your distance!' commanded Janet warningly, and with more vigour than she felt. The soldiers stood still, though one of them smiled unpleasantly, his eyes running over Isobel's tall figure, graceful beneath the plaid.

'Someone in authority shall know of what we've seen today,' Isobel put in with reckless courage, aware that this might simply increase their danger. But the soldiers were quite untroubled by the threat, and merely laughed derisively.

'Do you think they'd care?' one returned. 'After the trouble these savages have given us, anything goes.'

'What have those women and children ever done to you?' demanded Isobel indignantly.

'Now, don't tell me they don't know about the rebellion! Don't tell me they didn't wave their men off to follow the Pretender with all good wishes for his success! If their men weren't rebels, they'd be down there protecting their women, wouldn't they now?'

Before Isobel could protest further, a second soldier dug his companion in the ribs.

'We're wasting time—come on!' and he took a step towards them.

'You lay a hand on us and you're in trouble,' warned Janet. 'I'm no rebel, and nor is Mrs MacLean here.'

'Then what are you doing here, I'd like to know—'
began the soldier, but his companion cut him short.

'Mrs MacLean did you say? That wouldn't be the Mrs
MacLean who's wife to MacLean of Ardshee, would it
now?'

'What if it is?' asked Janet defensively.

'I reckon our Captain would like a word with you,'
said the soldier with a smirk of satisfaction. The disappointment of the other two men was clear, but the
women heard him with relief. That at least offered some
respite from whatever fate the soldiers had in mind for
them.

This was not how Isobel had dreamed of coming home,
marched between two soldiers, her arms harshly gripped, down the slope where the runner had carried the
fiery cross on that summer night last year. The third
soldier walked beside Janet, but without holding her, as
if with respect for her civilised appearance.

Just before the slope of the hill levelled out to the
headland there was a smooth knoll, edged on one side by
the woods which covered the cliffs, and giving a clear
view of the bay and the castle alike. Here they paused,
the soldiers scanning the busy scene for their commanding officer, Isobel and Janet feeling only deeper horror
as the small details of the looting and murder and rape
became clearer. A new dimension was added to their
distress as they watched, for red flames shot up suddenly
from the thatch of the nearest cottage, crackling brightly
through the dry heather stems. They were firing the
houses, and their Captain was personally supervising the
operation a short distance away.

One of the soldiers ran to tell him of their find, and he
turned, unsmiling but gratified, to meet the prisoners.
He was a tall spare man in a powdered wig, very smart in
his scarlet coat and tricorne hat. There was an excited
sparkle of anticipation in his eyes as he strode onto the
knoll and stood before Isobel and raised his hat.

'So you have come home, Mrs MacLean,' he greeted
her, in quiet yet familiar tones.

It was John Campbell the respected lawyer and trusted friend who faced her in all the magnificence of military scarlet.

Isobel stood transfixed with astonishment and disbelief, aware almost of an illogical and yet comforting conviction that now they would be safe and all would be well. Yet what logic was there in thinking that, when her eyes told her that John Campbell was responsible for all that they had seen this morning? She gazed at him in confusion and could think of nothing to say.

'Does your husband know you are here?' John asked in the same amiably conversational tone. She shook her head, and saw that he was faintly disappointed by her reply. 'Then you have not seen him since the battle?'

She shook her head again.

'I think he may be dead,' she added with difficulty, between dry lips.

'Indeed? What makes you think that?'

'A . . . a feeling,' she replied evasively, recognising that in an odd way it was almost a hope. She had seen enough today to know Hector could expect no mercy at John's hands.

'Ah, but I think he will come back here,' John went on, smiling a little. 'You came to wait for him, did you not?'

She nodded, frightened as once before by the odd light in his eyes.

'Then you shall do exactly as you planned, my dear, and sit at home to greet him on his return. We had meant to destroy the castle, but you must have a roof to shelter that pretty head. And I don't doubt we'll find some comfortable concealment there too while we wait. We shall all be ready to give Ardshee the welcome he deserves on his return. There's to be no quarter given to any rebel, you see, Isobel.'

Isobel shivered, but raised her head defiantly.

'I'll have no part in any plan of yours,' she returned. John raised an eyebrow quizzically.

'No? I think you will, my dear, I think you will.' He turned to the soldier who stood at Janet's side. 'Take the servant to the castle, and see she's well cared for. She's done no harm, and she can go home when an escort is available.' Isobel glimpsed Janet's face as they led her away, full of mingled amazement and rage and disgust, and above all a naked loathing for the gentlemanly Mr Campbell whom she had believed, once, to be worthy of her liking and respect.

'Now—' said John, as they were left with only the two soldiers for company. 'Now let's see what is to be done.'

Isobel knew, with sudden clarity, not only that she was very afraid, but also that whatever John threatened, whatever he did to her, he would not bend her to his will.

'I promised once to make you a widow again,' he went on, 'and I shall keep that promise. Sadly, I did not meet with Ardshee on Drummossie Moor—Culloden, as his Highness the Duke is pleased to call the battlefield—and I must admit I do not know his fate, except that there was no report of his death. But if he is alive he will, in time, come back here, will he not? I think you yourself have argued along those lines, or you would not be here now.' He paused for her answer, but none came and he continued smoothly. 'I had planned to lie concealed until he came, but the difficulty is that if he is as cautious as he ought to be, it might be difficult for us to lay hands on him once he sees the—er—disarray—' His hand indicated the burning settlement. 'On the other hand, were he to find you living peacefully here, mourning the dead but explaining that the trouble is past, and welcoming him warmly as a loving wife should—and were I and some others to lie concealed in the castle—then we would have him as neatly as a salmon on a hook. I think you will agree that your return is most apt, in the circumstances.'

'I shall do nothing, nothing at all, to help you,' Isobel asserted, and then added: 'And what if he is dead? You will have a long wait.'

'If he is dead, then word will come to Ardshee. And then, my dear,' he caressed her chin with his hand, though she drew sharply away, 'then, my dear, you will be mine. If Ardshee can force you to marriage, then so can I. And after all he did you came to care for him a little. It could happen again.'

'Never!' she lashed out. 'I'd sooner die!'

'Be careful,' he warned. 'I might take you at your word.'

'Then do!' she flung back at him. 'I meant what I said. You will never hurt Hector through any act of mine— and you will never have me as long as I live!'

John grasped her arms, and she was reminded forcibly of their last angry meeting. But now he spoke softly.

'Do not think you can protect Ardshee, Isobel. I have sworn to kill him, and I shall kill him, if he lives still. I swore it before ever I met you, for what his father did to mine. When he took you from me that only made me the more determined. And never think either that I want you for your fortune alone. Once perhaps that was true—but not for very long now, not for years. No, Isobel, you were meant to be mine, and one day I shall have you, as surely as this hand will strike down Hector MacLean and make you a widow.'

She looked into his eyes, and recognised the utter ruthlessness there. She had thought Hector ruthless, taking her in anger when she spurned him, trying by force and subtlety alike to lay his hands on her fortune. But she knew that John Campbell's ruthlessness was that of a madman, obsessed by desire for her and hatred for the man who had married her. She knew there was no appeal she could ever make to him with any faint hope of success. All she could do was to try and convince him that she could never be his, even by threats and violence.

'I shall not do as you ask, John,' she said quietly. 'Instead I shall do all in my power to see that Hector escapes you, if he is alive. There are many ways of warning him of his danger.' She hoped she sounded more confident than she was, not being at all sure how she would be able to protect her husband from this madman. But if, as she feared, he were dead, then it was unlikely she would ever be put to the test.

John's grasp tightened on her arms, and he brought his face close to hers, the eyes half-demented.

'What can he possibly mean to you, you little fool? He doesn't care for you, and he never will. You will never win his heart. What is more if he is alive now he will not live long even if he escapes me. There will be no mercy for the rebels this time, Isobel. You will never be able to live with him again. Have I not far more to offer? Respect, a good name, the regard of your parents, the knowledge of the world, even something of a reputation as a soldier now—think, Isobel, think what you could have. Help me that little I ask, and then you will be free—free to be mine.'

'Free! That's not freedom! Marriage to a man who can boast of his military reputation, after what I have seen today? No, John Campbell, death would be a better fate than that kind of freedom. Let go of me—I despise you now, and I shall despise you for ever, as long as I live!'

She saw his face livid with rage, and he flung her from him to fall on the ground at his feet, and called to the soldiers.

'Bind her!' he ordered. 'Bind her fast to that tree! We'll see if other means will win her, if fair words fail—'

They dragged her back against a tall pine and began to bind her roughly to the trunk. She struggled wildly, but John only laughed angrily and urged on the soldiers to use her less gently still.

'That's the way to tame a woman—beat her into submission!' he encouraged them savagely. She bit her lip so as not to cry out in fear and pain at their rough handling.

And then just as she braced herself to face whatever horror he had in store for her a wild figure leapt past her from the trees and a sword flashed out and one of the soldiers fell moaning with blood pouring from his head.

She felt the ropes about her arms tighten briefly, and then fall raggedly severed to the ground. Other hands dragged her from behind and thrust her into the trees.

'Run!' came the urgent command in Gaelic, and she ran, blindly obedient, into the woods, stumbling on stones and roots, pushing through branches that whipped her face and pulled at her clothes, deeper and deeper into the trees. The sound of shouts and clashing swords and a swift rattle of musket fire followed her, grew fainter, and died away. Steps crashed after her through the undergrowth and she did not know whether they were those of friends or pursuers.

At last she collided with a tree and leant against it, her breath coming in sobbing gasps. Her legs could carry her no further, though she heard footsteps close behind her. She turned, weakly—and the face which looked into hers was that of her husband.

'Hector!' she whispered, incredulous joy leaping through her. 'Oh, Hector!'

She reached out her arms to cling to him, and he took a step backwards, and the harsh cold light in his eyes turned her joy to ice.

'God damn you, woman,' he spat at her. 'Why did you have to come back? My brother is dead—and you have killed him!'

CHAPTER
FIFTEEN

ISOBEL'S first utterly inconsequential thought was that she had been foolish to think it mattered in the least how she looked to meet Hector again. For if it had not been for that instinctive leap of recognition in her heart she would scarcely have known her husband. There was no trace now of the splendid Highlander who had parted from her on the beach, or left in anger that last night. The man who faced her at this moment was well past caring how she looked.

Thin and haggard, his jawline etched with a black stubble beneath the too prominent cheekbones and the shadowed eyes, he looked like a man who had gazed too long on horrors. A dirty bloodstained bandage bound his head over the unruly hair, and there was blood, too, on the torn plaid which was all he wore over his ragged shirt, once so fine. His deerskin shoes were almost in pieces and fresh blood was trickling down his bare leg towards the tartan hose. Isobel felt a surge of pitying love, a longing to draw him into her arms and care for him with all the tenderness at her command. But the hate in his eyes and in his voice stood between them like an impenetrable barrier.

Slowly, inexorably, his accusing words sank into her numbed brain.

'What do you mean?' she whispered, sick with shock, her voice trembling. She watched that supple beloved mouth, that mouth which had met hers once with warmth and passion, tighten further into a bitter line.

'Hugh is dead.' The words fell one by one, sharp-edged, like deadly arrows piercing her heart. 'Dead because of you! They blew his head to pieces with musket shot as he ran to set you free. My brother—dead for *you*!'

She had not thought it was possible for one word to contain so much venom. '*You*', he said, as if she were utterly beneath contempt, as if she were some loathsome insect fit only to be crushed underfoot. She backed further against the tree, recoiling from the hate which was destroying her piece by piece as no violence could ever do. From somewhere within her shaking frozen body she found her voice.

'But I did not ask him to save me,' she whispered, her eyes imploring him to understand. 'I think he did not even like me.'

'No, he did not, and God knows he had reason! It was not for you he did it, never think that—it was because you are my wife, though I curse the day I ever saw you. Why did you come back? Why did you not stay with your own kind where you belong?' His anguished bewilderment moved her even as it crushed her spirit.

'Because . . . because . . .' she faltered, the words 'I love you' withered and dying, unspoken, beneath the cold hatred of his eyes. She pressed her palms against the rough bark of the tree, as if to seek strength from its ancient lichened trunk, but she could think of nothing to say. And then she realised for the first time that another Highlander stood a few paces away, awed into silence until now when he heard what Hector and Isobel were too distracted to notice. He grasped Hector's arm.

'The soldiers!' he whispered hoarsely, and Hector raised his head, listening.

The crash of feet through the undergrowth, a distant flash of scarlet glimpsed through the trees, warned them the soldiers were after them still. With icy urgency Hector pulled Isobel from against the tree and gave her a little push.

'Run, quickly—lead the way, Duncan.'

Isobel saw that he drew his dirk from his belt as he turned to follow them. It seemed to be the only weapon he had left.

The other man ran first, slipping neatly between the

trees, light-footed, sure of his path. Isobel alone made much sound as they passed through the bright dappled sunlight of the green spring wood, slithering on the steep slope, torn by brambles, tripping on fallen branches. Once Hector's hand grasped her elbow, steadying her as she crossed a stream where the ground fell sharply with no trees to break a fall. But the hand was withdrawn as quickly once the danger was past, and she knew that only practical necessity had driven him to touch her.

Behind them their pursuers were no longer in sight and before long silence fell over the wood, but for their own quiet progress, and they knew they were out of immediate danger. But they kept on at the same unflagging pace, until a soft grunt of satisfaction from Duncan indicated that they had reached their goal.

Here a vast jagged outcrop of rock ran steeply down the cliff face to the sea just visible through the trees far below. Moss and fern and a few thin trees covered it, and at its steepest point a narrow split gaped black in the grey-green of the rock. Isobel watched as Duncan slid into the space and signalled to her to follow.

It was too small to be termed a cave, a horizontal fissure just wide enough for three people to lie cramped and huddled behind the delicate veil of ferns. Isobel followed Duncan's example and crouched forward on her elbows with knees drawn up, gazing out over the steep drop to the sea, Duncan on one side and Hector on the other.

They lay panting and silent as the cold and damp of earth and rock cooled them and stiffened cramped limbs, and the wood settled into tranquillity about them.

Isobel was aware of every bone of Hector's body against hers, thinner and more angular than she remembered from the last time she had felt its closeness, though now the plaid softened its sharp lines. She longed desperately to turn her head and brush shoulder or cheek with her lips, to make some little gesture of tenderness, but one glance at his expression, dark and grimly impenetrable, defeated her. She guessed what his response would be, and what that would do to her.

To keep herself from thinking, to dull the ache in her heart, Isobel began to look about her as far as possible from her uncomfortable vantage point. Duncan, on her other side, was, she realised, as haggard and unkempt as his chieftain, though his square build masked his state a little. She could not remember him clearly, but thought she had seen his face once or twice among Hector's followers. Now, as the hours passed, his burly shoulders and brown bearded head became as familiar to her as the delicate lines of the ferns growing before her face, the vivid green of the moss at the cave mouth, the silver-grey line of a birch stem a little further off.

They spoke scarcely at all as they crouched in their uncomfortable hiding place. Clearly, talk overheard would give them away were the soldiers to search the wood, but Isobel sensed that neither Hector nor Duncan had much to say. Hector at least was lost in some gloomy thoughts of his own, and she dared not intrude. And when he did speak at last he revealed clearly enough what was uppermost in his mind.

'When it grows dark,' he murmured in an undertone, 'I shall go back to Ardshee.'

Isobel gave a low protesting cry; and then wished she had not when he turned those burning hate-filled eyes on her again.

'What is it to you if I do?' he retorted. 'I cannot leave my brother to lie there with no one to close his eyes and say a prayer over him. And you do not know what the soldiers did to the bodies of the dead on Drummossie Moor.' He spoke as if her ignorance on that score only increased her guilt.

'But they will kill you!' she protested.

'And what if they do? You will be free, will you not?' The cruel irony of his tone hurt her the more for its echoes of John's words a few hours before. 'I must know, too,' he went on more calmly, 'what has become of the people. God grant the soldiers have left them alone.'

'Did you not see?' Isobel asked, and then regretted the question, because of the inevitable response.

'Did I not see what? Tell me!' he commanded.

It was not easy. To find the words was hard enough, for her months at Ardshee had not taught her the Gaelic for 'rape' and 'murder', and she could not bring herself to lapse into English, as if to do so would only underline the horror of it all. Worse still was to see the growing pain in Hector's eyes as he listened, and know that his suffering had been almost past bearing without this. When she had finished he bent his head in silence to the ground so that his face was hidden by his arms, and only the whiteness of his clenched knuckles showed what he endured. She knew there was no comfort she could offer.

She heard Duncan's murmured exclamation at her other side, and remembered that he, too, must have loved ones at Ardshee. She turned her head and saw that his blue eyes were full of unshed tears, in a silent, anguished appeal for help.

'My woman . . .' he whispered brokenly, 'and the little ones . . .' Isobel laid her hand over his and held it, glad that even so small a gesture seemed to bring him a measure of comfort. At least here she was not helpless. But she knew how inadequate a response it was to what had happened today.

There was no more talk, and the day wore on. The sun disappeared and a cold wind rustled through the trees and stirred the ferns over their hiding place. Hector remained as he was, motionless and silent, and at one point Duncan fell asleep, though how he could sleep in so uncomfortable a position Isobel did not know. She knew that Hector's immobility was not that of slumber.

Much later, gazing down at the water below, grey as the rocks that edged it now that the sun had gone, Isobel watched idly as a heron stood fishing and then rose, suddenly startled, and flapped its slow way out of sight. It was a moment or two before she realised that what had disturbed it was the approach of a file of men along the shore, their scarlet coats gleaming against the slate-colour of the sea.

'Hector!' she whispered urgently.

He raised his head, but she had no time to be shocked
at the new greyness of his face.

'Look!' she said, pointing below.

He nodded, and said nothing, narrowing his eyes to
watch them more intently. They both kept absolutely
still, and beside them their alertness communicated
itself somehow to Duncan and he awoke and watched,
motionless in his turn.

The soldiers, about a dozen of them, marched untidily
along the shore, away from Ardshee, and were lost to
sight.

Hector lay still for a moment longer, listening for any
warning sound, and then relaxed a little.

'I think they'll not trouble us,' he commented softly
after a pause. 'Perhaps they hope to find other prey
along the shore—may the Evil One send a wave to
drown them!'

'Could they be going to search the wood from the
other end?' Duncan asked tentatively.

For an instant all three had a clear mental picture of
themselves in their hiding place in the middle of the
wood as the soldiers advanced from either end, trapping
them irrevocably. And then Hector began to question
Isobel as to how many soldiers she had seen at Ardshee
this morning, and to calculate how thoroughly they
would be able to search the woods.

'I think they will not be able to cover the ground well
enough to find us,' he reassured them at last. 'And they
are noisy searchers. We should hear them coming a long
way off, and could climb out that way.' He pointed
above their heads, and Isobel hoped fervently that there
would be no need to scale that slippery rock face. 'They
have the ship keeping watch from the sea, of course, but
they will not have men enough to surround the wood as
well as search through it. We shall be safe, God willing.'

They fell silent again, straining for the first warning
sounds of an approaching search party. But none came.
The birds sang on, small animals rustled through the
undergrowth, the wind stirred the slender branches
above them. Distantly the waves swished and lapped on

the shore. When they did hear a new sound, it was not the one they had expected and feared.

Isobel's attention was caught first as Hector raised his head higher, suddenly alert. Far off, faint and indistinct, she thought she could hear an odd crackling sound. She could not be sure which direction it came from, nor what caused it. There was something familiar about it, but she could not think what.

'Smoke!' whispered Duncan, when they had listened for some time longer. They sniffed, and the smell was brought clearly on the wind, the acrid fragrance of burning wood.

Hector slid from the hiding place and stood up, gazing back in the direction of Ardshee from which the wind carried the smell.

'They've set the trees alight,' he told them, bleakly matter-of-fact.

Duncan and Isobel joined him, gazing in horror at the dark haze of smoke distantly visible, coming steadily nearer, shot with crimson tongues of fire licking at the trees, setting them spitting and crackling and shrivelling to blackness.

'We'll have to go that way!' cried Isobel, turning towards the east. She had already taken several steps when Hector grasped her arm.

'Look,' he said.

That way, too, the flames leapt among the branches, progressing less quickly because the wind was against them, but the cliff face curved a little there, shutting out the force of the breeze, and the soldiers had done their job well.

'So they need very few men,' commented Hector. 'Just enough to watch up above, and some stationed on the ship, with guns perhaps.' Again he spoke without emotion, as if nothing he said was of any importance. Fighting a growing panic, Isobel cried out;

'What are we going to do?'

He turned to her in surprise.

'There is only one thing we can do. You do not swim, I think?' She shook her head. 'Then we go that way.'

He gestured upwards. Isobel felt the colour drain from her face.

'But you said they'd be watching,' she objected.

'We have no alternative,' he told her grimly, and she knew he was right. But she was not comforted by the feeling that he did not care very much either way.

At least they did not take the most difficult route over the rock face. Hector led the way this time, a little to the east of the rock, and Duncan came behind, ready to help Isobel should she need it. But though they had branches and grass to help their climb, and some reassurance in the thickly growing trees behind them, the cliff face was almost vertical at times, and even the sure-footed Highlanders found the climb slow and difficult.

And all the time the flames crept steadily closer. Above, Isobel guessed, the soldiers would be watching the pall of smoke, estimating when they could expect to see the fugitives run into the open, caught like rabbits at harvest time. And this time she knew John Campbell would make sure of his prey.

It was a terrible climb for Isobel, her legs trembling and aching with the unfamiliar exercise, slithering on smooth grass, struggling to find one foothold and then another, her weight dragging on arms which reached out for this branch or that rock, or for Hector's hand stretched down to pull her to safety. And all the while knowing that a greater danger awaited them at the end.

Close to the summit Hector paused, and signalled to them to do the same.

'Wait there,' he ordered. 'I'm going on to see which is the best way.'

He was gone only a few minutes, but they seemed like hours to Isobel, supported on the grassy slope to which she clung, with Duncan anxiously watching below. She began to fear the sound of shots, and the realisation that Hector would never come back. And then his head appeared again, just above her.

'This way,' he whispered. 'Follow me, and do exactly as I say.'

They followed him onto a grassy ledge where a little

spring trickled sideways to form a long silver thread of waterfall to the rock face below. It made its way towards them along a narrow gully, scarcely as broad as Hector's shoulders, but running nearly three feet into the earth. The trees sheltered it on either side, but they could see that further on it ran out into the open grass and heather of the hilltop.

Ahead of them Hector slid on his belly along the floor of the gully, heedless of the water running beneath him. By the time he followed the bed of the stream was thick and muddy, but Isobel knew better than to protest. She crept along at Hector's heels, scratched by protruding stones, quickly slimed with mud and soaked through to the skin. Duncan followed her as silently.

It could not have been very far that they moved in this slow and uncomfortable manner, but it felt like miles. Now and then Hector left them again for a moment to see that the way was clear before they went on, and then the horrible progress—a slither rather than a crawl—was resumed.

At last the gully grew shallower, and came to an end by a knot of wind-blown pines towering overhead. Hector stopped, turned his head briefly and whispered: 'Into the heather!' and then pulled himself out of the gully beneath the trees.

Blindly Isobel and Duncan followed. The heather was scarcely growing yet, and gave little cover, but in spite of the fear and discomfort Isobel reflected briefly that a dirty plaid provided ideal dress for concealment among the rough browned stems.

They crawled as before, but dry now, their skin rubbed raw by the harsh heather roots. And now of course there was no gully to hide them, only their ability to move as smoothly and neatly as snakes over the bleak landscape. And Isobel knew that she had no ability of that kind at all, though the Highlanders had been trained to it from birth.

They had gone forward in this way for about a hundred yards when a shot whistled low over their heads.

'Lie still!' came Hector's hoarse command, and they

froze, motionless, listening for another shot. But none came, though they heard the distant sound of shouting: question, answer, an order. After a little while Hector whispered 'Come on' and they moved forward again, more cautiously this time.

Isobel kept her head lower than before, and surreptitiously pulled a fold of the plaid over her hair, for fear its golden brightness would betray them. She was aware, horribly, that they were moving steadily nearer to the shouting soldiers.

They had gone only a few yards more when the shots came again, missing them by inches, a volley this time sending Isobel flat on her face in panic, as if the earth could open and hide her if she clung close enough. And then Hector shouted 'Run!'

For a second she hesitated, but no more. As Duncan passed her she scrambled to her feet and ran in a second hail of shots after Hector's flying figure. From the corner of her eyes she saw the dark shapes of three soldiers running towards them over the heather, some way off yet.

Ahead was a slight rise, split by another gully, deeper than the first. Hector made straight for it, and they followed, stumbling, moving with all the speed their weary bodies could muster.

Hector had come to the gully, flinging himself forward into it, and then in agony Isobel saw a soldier take shape on the slope above and level his musket.

'Hector!' she shrieked.

Just in time he saw, and the shot missed, and she saw him leap up the slope after the soldier, his dirk in his hand. She paused, her heart in her mouth, and Duncan seized her arm.

'Come!' he urged, and she ran with him. They reached the gully just as the soldier fell and Hector sprang down after them.

Behind them the other three soldiers were coming quickly nearer, though they did not pause to fire. Two more were running to join them from the other direction. The pounding of their feet sounded suddenly loud on the hard earth between the high sides of the gully.

'We can't escape!' Isobel thought in panic. Their pursuers were gaining on them, and she knew her legs could not carry her much further. She felt Hector's hand on her arm, pulling her with him, and some of his strength reached her, urging her on. A shot rang out, and she heard Duncan give a low cry, but he was running with them still.

Their pursuers were close behind them now, the gap was closing. Just as Isobel knew she must fall to her knees and rest a soldier flung himself over the final distance and sent Hector flying to the ground. Isobel screamed.

She was thrust aside, helpless as Duncan grappled with another man and Hector rolled over and over in the grip of his assailant, struggling desperately to free himself enough to pull his dirk from his belt. He had it once and then she saw the soldier's hand close about his wrist and the dirk fell from his grasp. Quick as lightning she seized it, and raised it over the soldier's back. And as quickly she was grabbed from behind and pulled clear, the dirk thrown into the dust.

But that momentary scuffle gave Hector his chance. For an instant his assailant was distracted, and Hector slid free. He had the dirk in his hand then, and the blade flashed out to meet the soldier's chest as he sprang towards Hector. He fell and did not rise again.

Shots flew over Isobel's head, but Hector seized the dead soldier's musket and returned the fire. Isobel heard the man behind fall with a grunt, and saw Hector turn coolly to shoot Duncan's attacker. Then he ran to the high ground above the gully watching as the two last soldiers came running towards them. One more shot and one of them lay still while the other fled.

'They'll be back,' Hector assured them. He was struggling painfully for breath, Isobel noticed, and even in the dusk she could see the perspiration damp on his pale face. As for her, she longed to sink to the ground, but knew she would not be able to rise again if she did.

'Come,' panted Hector relentlessly, and set out at a

steady loping run whose speed astonished Isobel after all
he had been through. Without a word she and Duncan
followed his example. Once well into its rhythm, she
found, it was easy enough, in spite of weariness, to keep
up the pace.

It was nearly dark when Hector stopped at last. The
dim light showed them a knot of trees and some kind of
half-ruined stone building, and he led them towards it.

'We'll rest here,' he said.

There was no door, and little left of the roof, but it
gave Isobel an overwhelming sense of shelter and security to sink down on the weed-grown earth floor with her
back against the wall and close her eyes. She felt she
would never be able to move again, even to raise her
hand. She was aware of Duncan and Hector sinking
down near her into the same exhausted immobility. For
a long time there was complete silence.

It was Hector who broke it at last, saying in a slow
subdued tone which betrayed his weariness,

'I shall go back to Ardshee soon, when it grows fully
dark.'

Even Duncan exclaimed at that, and Isobel found the
strength to open her eyes and turn towards Hector, still
slumped against the wall at her side.

'You cannot go back!' she protested. 'Not after all that
has happened.'

'It makes no difference at all,' he returned with weary
unconcern. 'Besides, we need food.'

Food! With a sudden flash of recollection Isobel remembered the leather pouch fastened securely beneath
her plaid. It was still there—she felt it now—and in it lay,
along with her money, the barley bread and cheese
remaining from that meal eaten in the happy optimism
of the dawn. It seemed extraordinary to think that it was
still the same day.

'I've got some food,' she said. 'Bread and cheese. I'd
forgotten it until now.' She saw the eyes of the two men
turn on her with an eager light which surprised her.
'There isn't much,' she added cautiously, and bent to
pull the now crushed and crumbled food from the pouch.

Certainly there was little enough, but at least as it had been her turn to carry the food, she had Janet's share as well as her own, so there would be something to keep them going. She was about to divide it into three portions when some instinct made her pause.

'When did you last eat?' she asked Hector. He hesitated before replying, clearly making some elaborate mental calculation.

'It would be the day before the battle,' he said slowly at last. 'We had a biscuit each, I remember. Though one day, too, a woman gave us a bannock—somewhere in Lochaber I think it was—and we have drunk, of course. There is always water.'

Isobel gazed at him in horror. It must be about four days now since the battle. And today at least he had run from the soldiers, and fought them to save her, and fought again just now, and there had been that climb—she marvelled at the strength and endurance of these Highlanders. And she carefully broke all the bread and cheese into two and gave an equal portion to each of them.

Duncan began to eat at once, mumbling his thanks over the first eager mouthful, but Hector paused.

'You have none for yourself,' he pointed out quietly.

'I have eaten today,' she told him. Then she tried not to shame him by watching as slowly and carefully he began to eat. Afterwards he only said with grave courtesy: 'I thank you for that, Isobel,' and went to the broken doorway to look out on the darkening landscape.

Now, Isobel thought, perhaps they could sleep, ready to go on in the morning. It was too dark now for more than to make out her companions as darker shapes in the shadow. Hector stood outlined against the deep blue of the night sky, a motionless black figure.

At last he turned.

'It is time I went now,' he said.

'But there is no need!' cried Isobel. 'You have eaten now—we can go on in the morning.'

'You forget why I have to go,' he reminded her. Remembering, and knowing how he blamed her, Isobel could not tell him how ridiculous she thought him. 'I can see how they are, too, and bring them news, though my heart is heavy at the thought—'

'Let me go,' broke in Duncan eagerly. 'My Catriona is there, and the children—' He began to rise and then fell back, moaning a little. Isobel remembered suddenly how he had cried out as he ran.

'I think he may have been hit,' she said quickly.

They lifted him to the doorway where they could see more clearly. He was already trying to sit up, but a musket ball had grazed his arm and it was clear he had lost a great deal of blood. Isobel tore a strip from her petticoat and bound it tightly about the wound.

'He needs rest,' she told Hector, 'and so do you. I think we should all stay here for the night. It can do no good to go back to Ardshee.'

'I shall go when I'm rested,' added Duncan from the floor.

'I am going now,' said Hector, totally ignoring their intervention. They might as well not have spoken, thought Isobel, tight-lipped.

'Duncan,' he went on, 'if I am not back by dawn you must take Mrs MacLean to my uncle Ranald MacDonald in Glencoe. He was too old to be out so it should be safe there, and he will see that my wife returns to her parents—but I shall be back.' And with that he was gone.

CHAPTER
SIXTEEN

'How can he be so foolish!' exclaimed Isobel in an exasperated tone when Hector's black shape had been swallowed up in the greater darkness of the mountainside. But it was not mere exasperation which tore at her heart. 'He will walk straight into the soldiers.'

'I think they will not be watching now,' Duncan consoled her slowly. 'Nor will they be expecting him. And he was always skilled at following the deer.'

Which activity brought no possible danger to his life, thought Isobel, but there was some comfort in Duncan's words.

She heard him murmur some prayer or charm and settle himself to sleep, and then sat for a long time gazing through the broken roof at the few stars which showed through the clouds, trying to make some sense of the day in her tired brain. So much had happened, so many terrible things, and yet now she felt only numbed. She recognised that most of all exhaustion robbed her of the power to feel or think. Perhaps it was just as well.

In the end she fell asleep on the hard cold earth and slept soundly for what might have been hours or might have been only minutes. It was still dark when she awoke, and it was raining, a fine steady drenching rain without wind, blotting out stars and landscape alike.

She reached over to reassure herself that Duncan was under the intact portion of the roof where the rain could not reach him, and then drew back herself against the wall at his side. He was deeply asleep, snoring gently, but she herself felt alarmingly wide awake and clear-headed.

The past day seemed now like a bad dream. She could not really believe that it had all happened, above all that

Hector had turned on her with those terrible eyes and
cursed her for his foster-brother's death. She could not
believe that when he returned he would ever look at her
like that again, now they had shared a common danger
and escaped it together.

If he returned. For that fear at least was real. She drew
her knees up to her chin and closed her eyes and prayed
fervently for his safe return.

The first hesitant greyness of the dawn had lightened
the clouds when Hector slipped silent as a shadow into
their hiding place. Isobel had not heard him coming,
alert though she was to every sound.

He did not look at her, simply went to Duncan and
knelt at his side to make sure he was well. Isobel did not
dare to ask him what he had found at Ardshee, for she
could not see his face well enough to judge his mood.
She wondered fleetingly if he had forgotten she was
there.

She heard him shake Duncan gently awake, and when
the older man sat up, rubbing his eyes, tell him briefly
that his wife and children were alive and well.

'I cannot say more now,' he added. 'We must be on
our way before daylight.'

'Why is that?' broke in Isobel sharply. 'Surely the
soldiers will not be on us so soon?'

'They are camped about half a mile from here,' Hector told her without looking round. 'They were already
stirring when I passed, and it seems likely that they plan
to move forward to take us at first light. I think they will
not be certain we are here, but there are few enough
hiding places in these parts. We will be safer in the
open.'

Isobel felt her heartbeat quicken with alarm. She had
not somehow expected this new danger, though perhaps
she should have done. She had seen enough of John
Campbell's hatred of Hector to know he would not
lightly give up the pursuit.

They set out almost at once, pausing only to drink
from a burn near their ruined shelter before hurrying on
with Hector leading the way. It was already light enough

to make out the shapes of rocks and trees and the undulations of the landscape. It was also still raining steadily, and all three pulled their plaids well over their heads to provide some protection from the drenching wetness. Isobel noticed that Hector's clothes were already sodden. She hoped that Highlanders were by nature as impervious to the damp as they seemed to be to starvation and exhaustion. Hector appeared tireless even now, after a day and a night of almost continuous activity. For all she knew he had been walking and running since the battle.

They followed the burn down to where it ran into a small loch lying quiet and steel-grey, its surface pitted with rain, in a hollow of the hills. Hector led them around its edge, over rocky hummocks and miniature bays of fine sand, and onto the mountainside beyond.

After that there were few landmarks which presented themselves to Isobel, but only an apparently endless succession of tussocks of grass and patches of heather, varied with rocks and marshy places designed only to make the way more arduous. It seemed as if every summit they reached only led to another. The sole comfort was that there was neither sight nor sound of pursuit. It looked as if Hector's prompt action had saved them again. Even so they did not pause, and they moved as silently as if there were soldiers listening behind every stone.

At last they came to a small glen driven deep into the mountains and Hector led them to the inadequate shelter of a little wood.

'We shall rest here,' he said, in the toneless voice which he seemed to use all the time now. They crouched down where the trees grew most thickly, the two men side by side and Isobel a little way off. She knew it would be sensible to go closer, for warmth and shelter, but she was afraid to intrude where she was not wanted. Hector had not looked at her today as he had in that dreadful moment yesterday, but he had scarcely looked at her at all, and then without any trace of warmth. Now his first thoughts were for his other companion.

'Catriona is well, and the children too,' he said to Duncan. 'They are more fortunate than most, for they contrived by some miracle to escape the soldiers' attention—I think perhaps our coming was just in time to save one or two of them in the same way. So you can be comforted, and when it is quieter you will be able to go home. So long as we do not go back to Ardshee now I think they will be left in peace.'

Isobel saw Duncan bend his head on his hands in thankfulness at the news. But there was one urgent question Hector had not answered, and she burst out:

'Mairi—what of Mairi?'

Unmistakably, hatred lit Hector's eyes as he turned to her, and she recoiled as if he had struck her.

'She is dead, did you not know?' He spoke harshly, clearly expecting no answer. 'But of course you did not, for you had run away by then.'

'Then she was already dead when the soldiers came?' Isobel asked quickly, her own pain forgotten in her concern for the old woman. 'Oh, then I am thankful she was spared—'

'Perhaps it was her knowledge of my wife's unkindness which killed her,' returned Hector unpleasantly. 'I only know she died in January, and they brought me word of it. That was when I learned you had gone, and that you were to bear a child.' The cold eyes scanned her searchingly. 'You do not look as if that were true.'

'I lost the baby,' Isobel told him in a faltering whisper. Even now, after all that had happened, the memory pained her.

'That was one result of your flight from Ardshee I suppose? Then you killed my child as surely as you killed my brother.' He ignored her anguished protest and went on. 'Why did you come back? What possible reason could you have, in God's name? Did your parents refuse to take you in?'

She longed to tell him the truth, but feared the bitter contempt of his response. She said only, 'It was not that. But I . . . I did make a solemn vow, once, even if I was

forced to it . . . and . . . I wanted to show I was—
worthy—of you . . .'

He gave a harsh laugh, abrupt and utterly without
warmth.

'Oh you have shown it, Isobel MacLean, you have
shown it—only I wonder what I am to have deserved
you—'

'I did not choose to marry you, remember,' she reminded him, so close to tears that her voice sounded
rough and petulant, concealing the pain she felt.

'You did not, God help me,' he agreed bitterly. A
silence followed, uncomfortable and prolonged. It was
Duncan who broke it, placing his hand on Hector's arm.

'Your foster-brother Hugh—how is it with him?'

Hector turned away from Isobel, his expression at
once softer, full of a gentler grief.

'All is well with him now, Duncan. Thank God they
had not used his body as foully as they did those of the
dead on Drummossie Moor. The women will see to his
burying.'

'He was a good man,' added Duncan, and Hector
nodded his agreement. The older man went on, as if
reciting an old tale, 'He saved your life on Drummossie
Moor. When you fell with that wound to your head he
bore you on his back from the field and would not rest
until you were far from the fight. And he watched over
you to keep you from harm, and from the soldiers who
were killing the wounded.'

'And you watched with him,' Hector reminded him.

'What happened to the other men who went with
you?' Isobel asked.

Again that cold light gleamed in Hector's eyes. She
told herself she would not question him again.

'They died of course,' he answered now, 'with all the
hundreds who fell that day. If any lived I did not hear of
it.'

After a while their more immediate needs came to
mind, and she forgot her resolution to ask no more
questions and asked:

'Did you bring any food from Ardshee?'

Again came that unpleasant laugh.

'Food? Where do you imagine I would find food at Ardshee? The soldiers drove off the cattle before they left, and took everything else they could lay their hands on. We have your good friend John Campbell to thank for that.'

'You know he is no friend of mine!' she retorted, stung to indignation by his tone. 'You saw what he did to me—and it's because of him that I lost the baby.'

'That does surprise me!' Hector flung at her with harsh irony. 'I did not know he had such a hand in my wife's affairs. Did you enlist his aid to rid you of it?'

The injustice of his words stung her to anger.

'How can you say that? I know only too well what he is, to my cost.' She told him briefly how John had come to take her home, and then how she had learned the truth about him, and how his violence had brought on the miscarriage already threatened by the long journey. When she had finished she saw Hector's brows draw together fiercely and he burst out,

'Then I have more than I knew to charge him with— and he shall pay for all the wrong he has done. For taking you away from me. For the death of my unborn child. Above all for the death of my brother. For that I blame you, as for the other things, but John Campbell more even than you, for you are only a weak woman and it was his hand which fired the shot that killed my brother.'

All at once he pulled the dirk from his belt and fell onto his knees, and laid his hand over the gleaming blade, his eyes burning and terrible words pouring from him like liquid fire.

'I swear by the Trinity and the Blessed Saints that I shall seek John Campbell all my days until I find him, and that I shall end his life with my own hand. And if I fail in this may I be cursed in all I do, may I meet a coward's death and lie without burial in a strange land. So let it be to me.'

And as Isobel shivered with horror he rose to his feet, and slid the dirk back into his belt, and said:

'But first you must be taken to safety.'

She almost retorted that he owed her nothing, that she did not ask him to take care of her, knowing that he hated her as he did. And then she realised what his words implied. As long as he felt responsible for her, as long as she was with him, he would put aside his sworn intention to seek out John Campbell and kill him. And for so long therefore he would be safe from the soldiers who marched under John Campbell's orders, and who would imprison or kill him the moment he came near their Captain. So she said nothing, and rose to her feet in her turn to follow Hector on the next stage of this seemingly endless journey.

CHAPTER
SEVENTEEN

THE days fell into a dreary and repetitive pattern. Mile after mile of heather and grass and bog passed beneath their feet, their only rest when they huddled in cold and darkness in a wood or against a wall or anywhere that offered some prospect of shelter. They ate roots and plants, or once a little food given by a kindly Highland woman whom the soldiers had somehow missed. They drank from the burns. They were eaten in their turn by midges. When, now and then, Hector ordered a longer stay—a day or two perhaps—in some precarious hiding place, there was little chance of repose, with the need to be constantly watching for the approach of troops. And always it seemed to rain and rain almost without ceasing.

A glimpse of scarlet through trees, or the familiar sounds of soldiers at work, caused the only breaks in the routine of the days. They had learnt long since that John Campbell was not alone in wreaking a terrible vengeance on the rebels: Isobel thought they must have covered miles retracing their steps to avoid plundering troops of one regiment or another. She had lost all track of time, and had no longer any idea how long they had been travelling, or what day it was. She grew used to aching legs and sore feet, and when her shoes shredded away to nothing she walked barefoot like the two men and endured the discomfort without complaint. She was relieved at least that the gentler walking in Janet's company had prepared her a little for this.

But she knew she could cheerfully have borne any hardship if only Hector had shown her some little kindness greater than the cold disdainful courtesy of his manner towards her. She longed almost for the fire of his anger, as preferable to the chilling contempt which marked his every word and action. She was no more to him than a burdensome responsibility of which he must rid himself as soon as possible. But she did not ask him where he was taking her, for he so clearly wanted as little to do with her as he could. Only to Duncan did he choose to talk at all, and that not often.

One day, when it had rained even more than usual and the wind had blown since dawn with relentless force, they came on a cottage set by itself in a small glen on a lochside. They had eaten nothing of any substance for some days now, and Hector suggested they ask at the house for food and shelter.

They approached it together and knocked on the door, but when it opened at last suspicious eyes examined them through a narrow crack.

'What are you wanting?' demanded a man's voice. The hospitable courtesy Isobel had come to expect even from strangers among Highlanders was entirely lacking in his tone.

'We should be glad of an hour or two of rest, if you have a little space under your roof,' replied Hector. 'And if by chance you could spare us some food—'

The eyes looked them up and down, and then the man said:

'We have nothing for you. Go on your way and leave us in peace.'

As Hector opened his mouth to protest, the door was shut firmly in his face.

'God's curse on him!' muttered Duncan into his beard, but Hector laid a weary hand on his arm.

'We can do nothing. Let us go on.'

They were well on their way when a cry from behind caught their attention. A woman was running from the house towards them, waving a package in her hand.

'I am sorry,' she panted as she came up to them, 'for the unkindness of my husband, but he is afraid, you see, for myself and the children as well as for himself.'

'He was out with the Prince then?' Hector asked, but the woman shook her head.

'He is no rebel. But the soldiers do not ask before they

shoot. Two men of our clan were killed just three days ago, and the women attacked. And we are told that any who give aid to rebels are to be named as rebels themselves. So you see we have cause to be afraid. But,' she went on, 'here is a little meal, so that you will not go hungry.'

Hector took the package, breaking into warm thanks, but she stopped him.

'Take it, and go,' she said quickly, and ran back down the track to the house.

Hector watched thoughtfully as the door shut firmly behind her and silence descended again on the glen, but for the rain and wind. Then he turned without a word and led them on up the hillside.

They found a hollow where the full force of the wind did not quite reach and crouched there while Hector placed a little of the meal on a wide flat stone and mixed it to a paste with some water cupped in his hand from a burn, and gave it to them to eat. It was surprisingly satisfying, Isobel found, at least when one had not eaten for so long beforehand.

Afterwards Hector spoke to them with new decision.

'I had meant to take you, Isobel,' he said, 'to the house of my uncle Ranald MacDonald. If it had not been for the soldiers we should have been there by now. He is a very old man and in poor health, so he was not out with the Prince, and it had seemed to me that he might be able to arrange for you to be escorted safely back to your parents, without danger to himself. He would have been happy enough to assist in any scheme which might thwart John Campbell—'

'What has he to do with John Campbell?' Isobel interrupted in bewilderment.

'He is my mother's older brother,' was Hector's cryptic reply, and he almost smiled at her sigh of exasperation. 'That is not very clear, I know. You see, what lies between John Campbell and myself goes back a long way—'

'Then it is not just . . . because of . . .' she hesitated, not wanting to remind him too readily of his score against her. But it had never been far from his thoughts of course, and there was no alarming change in his expression.

'Because of Hugh, and of you? No, they are only the latest wrongs, Isobel. It is an old story. You have heard perhaps how when King James—grandfather to Prince Charles—was driven from his throne by William of Orange, the clans were slow to swear an oath of allegiance to the usurper? And how because the MacDonalds of Glencoe delayed the false Campbells came to their homes and, having broken their bread and sheltered them beneath their roofs, slaughtered them against all the laws of God and man? My mother and her brother Ranald were children then, my mother little more than an infant, and they escaped somehow and saw how the guest who had slept in their house killed their father and their mother and their older brother while they slept, without mercy. Later they took shelter in my father's house, for he was some kind of kin of theirs, a young man just entered into the chieftainship at Ardshee. When they grew older, my mother and my father were married, and for his wedding gift to her my father swore a solemn oath to kill the man who had slaughtered her parents. So it was that he and my uncle Ranald MacDonald went together to the house of Archibald Campbell and saw justice done.'

Isobel considered the grim story in silence for a moment, conscious of Hector's eyes on her face, watching her enigmatically. She remembered John Campbell's claim that Alan MacLean had killed his father 'during a cattle raid'. She had enough knowledge of Highland morality to suspect that Hector's father might well have helped himself to some of his enemy's livestock when he took his revenge. Did that mean, then—She raised her eyes to Hector's face.

'So it was John Campbell's father whom your father and uncle killed that day.'

'That is so,' agreed Hector.

'But surely,' Isobel continued earnestly, 'it should have ended there. Justice was done, as your parents saw it. Perhaps you could not be expected to like John Campbell, but it was not your quarrel or his.'

For a moment, very briefly, a faint smile lifted the corners of Hector's mouth, as if in acknowledgement of her Lowland naïvety.

'It is never as simple as that,' he pointed out. 'And it did not end there. Because of his father's death ruin came to John Campbell's family. They lost their lands, his mother died, he was sent to be brought up far from his home, knowing he must make his own way in the world. He grew up hating my father for bringing this upon him—'

'It was your uncle's doing, too,' she reminded him. 'And surely you had nothing to do with it yourself?'

'I was not born then,' he conceded. 'And my uncle even as a youth was sickly and often ailing. It fell on my father to lay the plan to kill Archibald Campbell, and it was his hand that struck him down. So you see, John Campbell had been taught to hate my name, and when we met whilst I was at the University—'

'The University!' she exclaimed, her interest in the story briefly swallowed up by this new revelation.

'At Edinburgh,' he enlarged. 'I was a student there for some months before my father's death.'

She gazed at him in astonishment, seeing him with new eyes. That, then, explained the books, and perhaps the wine-coloured coat in the chest. But it was strange to think of this wild young man with his primitive notions of justice and revenge working quietly at his studies in the civilised city of Edinburgh. Especially as he was now, a black beard growing thickly about his darkly-tanned face, his hair tangled, his clothes ragged, his brown feet bare.

'Mairi never spoke of it,' she said wonderingly.

'It was not important.' He looked faintly amused, as if he understood her surprise at finding that her savage husband also had claims to be a man of the world. Then the sparkle in his eyes died away, and he resumed his story.

'It was while I was there that I met John Campbell,

and from the first it was clear that he hated me. At that stage, though, it was not mutual—until I came to know him better, that is. There were one or two things—a game of cards, when he cheated, and the stakes were high—and there was a girl—' He broke off, lost in thought for a little while, and Isobel was astonished at the force of the jealousy which twisted her heart.

'A girl?' she asked, as casually as she could. But the careful tone drew a sharp glance from Hector, and she blushed. He observed her for a moment or two longer, his expression unreadable but discomforting, and then went on:

'She was very young, as I was then, but an heiress. I suppose I had no hope in her parents' eyes, though in hers I think it was different—but that's not to the point. John Campbell was already making a name for himself, among those who knew less of him than I had cause to do, and he was older, and wiser in the ways of the world—' He paused again, his expression brooding, remembering. Finally he said: 'I think now it was a good thing for her that she died before she could become his wife.'

It explained so much, thought Isobel. When he learned that it was John who had taken her from Ard-shee it must have seemed almost as if history repeated itself. Except that with her it had been different, for he had never wanted anything from her but her money, and she sensed from his manner that he had loved that girl in Edinburgh, long ago. With a new insight she guessed that it was the presence of John Campbell at her side in the orchard which had driven him to abduct her, more than any anger at her rejection of him, more even than his desire for her fortune. In marrying her he had taken some kind of revenge for the loss of the girl he had loved all those years before. It was not a reflection which she found consoling.

'The rest you know, of course,' he added in conclusion.

'Yes,' she thought, 'only too well.'

'Do you think,' she asked slowly, after a pause, 'that

he has given up the pursuit, and will leave us alone now?'

'What do you think?' he returned. There was no need for her to reply. 'I think only that he has lost us for the moment, God willing. He will never give up as long as he knows we are alive. But he is not the only man we have to fear, and that is why I shall not after all take you to Glencoe. You have seen how even the innocent are not safe—and my uncle is a known Jacobite, for all his infirmity. No, I think taking all together we should not put him at risk. Instead, we shall find a secure hiding place, depending on help from no one, and remain there until the worst is over and I can find a way to see you safe home myself. It is not what I wanted—the sooner you are off my hands the better—and this will only prolong it. But I cannot put my friends at risk for my convenience. So we shall have to endure each other's company for somewhat longer.' He sprang to his feet. 'As for you, Duncan, I see no reason why you should not at once make your way back towards Ardshee, and hide near there until you judge it safe to go home. I doubt if the soldiers will return, and they would not go all that way to seek you. And alone you will be far safer than in our company.'

'Who then will protect you, if I am gone?' demanded Duncan fiercely. Hector smiled and laid a hand on his arm.

'I know of a place where we can lie hidden so safely that we shall not need your protection. You have done all you can. Be content with that, and go home in peace.'

Duncan seized his hand.

'And what of you? What will you do when she—' he nodded towards Isobel— 'is safe and you have killed that evil man? Will you come home also?'

Hector shook his head, and the desolate sadness of his eyes pierced Isobel's heart.

'I think I may never come back to Ardshee,' he said slowly, his voice rough with emotion. 'If I do it will not be for many years. I can be of no help to you all any more, though it grieves me deeply to think it. Perhaps,' he ended in an undertone, 'it is just as well, for I have brought you nothing but grief.'

Duncan cried out in protest, but Hector silenced him.

'It doesn't matter, Duncan. Go home now. Tell them all, when you see them again, that I have them always in my heart. And take care.'

Duncan held Hector's hands in an anguished clasp.

'Blessings go with you.'

'And with you,' Hector replied, and the older man turned and walked briskly away, his head high, though Isobel thought he was weeping.

Hector's mood was one of black despair as they set out again. He said nothing at all to Isobel, but walked a few paces ahead of her lost in thought and more unapproachable than she had ever known him to be, even during the last bleak days. She could scarcely believe he had ever unbent enough to talk so easily and so naturally of his past.

She realised as the days went by that it was unlikely he would ever speak to her so confidingly again. The grim taciturnity became a part of him, something she came to accept and endure, like the midges which plagued them incessantly, except when the wind blew at its strongest. If Hector spoke to her at all it was to issue an instruction or to give her some advice, as briefly and as curtly as he could. He had told her she was an unwanted encumbrance, and he made it plain that this was exactly what he felt. More than once she was tempted to tell him to leave her to fend for herself, until she remembered why she decided to stay with him. That left her no course but uncomplaining acceptance of everything he asked of her.

The safe hiding place of which Hector had spoken to Duncan lay along a small river which wound its way between grassy banks in a ravine cut deep in a mountainside. Hector led Isobel at the river's edge, over soft emerald turf scattered with a glowing profusion of wild flowers, towards a point where the river bent into a thickly growing wood and disappeared.

Here trees ran from the skyline, brilliantly blue today, down the steep sides of the ravine to the river bank. The water flowed more swiftly nearer its source, and the ravine narrowed giving little space for them to find a way beside the sparkling water. The afternoon sun which had lain still and hot on the grass was far above them and the shadows were deep and cool under the trees. There was no visible path, but Hector simply followed the line of the river as it twisted and turned through the woods.

Then at last they rounded another curve of the water, and Hector stopped. Here, suddenly, the ravine widened again, and the trees ended, and a great curved rock face spread from side to side. And over it, roaring and tumultuous and sparkling in the sunlight, the river tumbled in a wide fall to a bubbling pool beneath.

Isobel gasped with delight at the unexpectedness of it. Hector merely walked on, round the edge of the pool where the rock formed a narrow shelf beneath the overhanging face above, until he came to the very edge of the fall. And then, as she watched, he disappeared beneath it.

Isobel followed, and saw that the narrow shelf continued behind the fall, gleaming and slippery with water. Clinging to the rock face she edged her way along it. And found herself all at once in a wide cave, completely concealed behind the plunging water.

The cave was wide and high enough for a tall man to stand upright inside, and lit with a gentle greenish light because of the trees and the water and the ferns which grew in the damp places at its mouth. It was also surprisingly dry. Isobel looked at Hector and caught a fleeting gleam of triumph in his eyes before he was immediately practical again,

'We should be safe here,' he said. And then: 'I suggest you rest. I shall not be long.'

And before she could say anything he had gone.

She watched him veiled by the silver curtain as he made his way back along the path and disappeared into the trees. Clearly any fugitive in the cave could see what went on outside without difficulty, while being completely hidden by that dramatic fall of water. Even in her present despondent state she was impressed. It would be hard to imagine a better place than this in which to hide.

Hector made several journeys carrying heather to the cave to make beds, and coldly declining Isobel's offers of help. She noticed how pointedly he heaped the two makeshift couches at opposite sides of the cave. It hurt her, but she accepted it, as she accepted everything, without comment or complaint.

Later, when the beds were ready, Hector gathered dry sticks and lit a small fire. Isobel watched in fascination as he laid a flat stone over the fire to heat, and then mixed oatmeal and water and shaped it into little cakes to bake on the hot stone. His lean brown fingers moved quickly and neatly, with the skill of long practice.

'You've done that before,' she observed quietly.

He looked up, as if he had been so lost in thought that until she spoke he had forgotten she was there.

'We learned to fend for ourselves when we were hunting in the hills,' he told her in his usual cool abstracted tones.

Isobel had a sudden longing to sting him into some kind of warmer response. Even anger would be better than this distant coldness, she thought.

'I suppose it was useful to be able to cook whilst out on your cattle raids,' she said pointedly. 'John Campbell told me all about that old Highland custom.'

'I am surprised John Campbell remembers so much of the Highland ways,' Hector retorted, with much less fire than she had hoped.

'Ah, then you did lift cattle now and then!' she said triumphantly.

'Not personally,' he returned casually, 'but they were lifted. What can you expect? Our cattle are our wealth. In your part of the world men steal gold. In the Highlands they steal cattle. I see little difference. Except that it is both more skilful and more dangerous to steal cattle, which is why the Highlanders are so renowned a race of warriors.' At that point he seemed to recollect suddenly where that renown had so recently brought his warrior race, and fell silent, his expression once more brooding and withdrawn.

Isobel was disappointed. She wandered restlessly about the cave until he told her the food was ready. They ate, as always, in silence, while outside the shadows deepened and the silver-green light faded to grey and then to dusky blue.

Afterwards, as he extinguished the last embers of the fire in case their glow should give them away in the dark, Hector said:

'We shall stay here for as long as I see fit. I can easily leave unobserved to seek food or news, should there be any, and I think we have as much comfort here as we can hope for at the present. When I am sure that the soldiers are less busy I will take you near enough to your home to be sure you arrive there safely.'

'But how do you know I want to go home?' she cried. 'You have not asked me.'

'I still do not understand why you ever came back, though I curse the day you did so. Or did you lie when you said it was not that your parents would not have you? If you did not, then I cannot imagine you would wish now to be anywhere else but with your parents. Do you?'

Isobel bent her head and thought how impossibly remote her parents seemed from all this. Even Ardshee seemed far away and unreal. How could she ever want to be anywhere but with Hector, after all she had been through to return to him?

But she had come back to him in the hope that she might win his love, and now she knew with chilling certainty that all her hope was illusory. He was further now from loving her than he had ever been. She had recognised long ago that she no longer attracted him as once she had done. She had never had any other hold on his affections. And she saw daily how little he wanted her.

No, she thought, I cannot go on like this, sharing his every moment but for ever shut out from the smallest corner of his mind and heart. I cannot go on loving and loving with no hope of return, knowing only that he wants above all to be rid of me. I cannot ask him, loving him as I do, to endure my hateful company for a moment longer than he must. I will stay with him to keep him safe as long as I reasonably can. And then I shall return meekly to my parents when he tells me to go, and pray that somehow he will come in the end to find safety and happiness without me.

She raised her head and gazed steadily at all she could see of him in the dimness.

'Yes of course,' she said gravely. 'I shall be glad to go home.'

CHAPTER
EIGHTEEN

THERE were some moments during the weeks passed in the cave which Isobel treasured as the nearest she was ever likely to come to happiness, knowing that the final parting lay ahead. The cave itself was a strange yet beautiful refuge in which that soft silver-green light bathed the simplest task in mystery, and the constant rush of the water closed them in together as if this place were the whole world. On fine days the water shimmered like a curtain of silver threaded with diamonds. When, more often, it was wet they scarcely knew, for the sound of the fall drowned all other sounds.

Sometimes Hector would swim in the deep dark-brown water beneath the fall, and Isobel would watch his lithe scarred body leaping and curving in the pool, as sinuous and beautiful as those of the seals she had watched sometimes from Ardshee. At other times he left her to seek food, bringing a rabbit he had snared, a small fish; once, triumphantly, a salmon on which they feasted for two days.

Often he seemed to have forgotten that she was anything other than a companion in adventure, as his clansmen would have been when out hunting in the glens. His manner towards her at such times was easy, courteous, and yet reticent. He rarely smiled, and never allowed any real warmth or intimacy to blossom between them, but it was better far than the bitter coldness which shut her out so completely when he remembered who she was and why she was there.

Once or twice he crept down under cover of darkness to some friendly cottage to beg a little meal or milk and ask for news. They heard that the soldiers marched less often through the glens these days. Most of the chiefs and other rebels who had not died at Culloden, or in the slaughter afterwards, were in prison now, awaiting trial in Carlisle or York or London, knowing that the victors were eager to see the gallows at work.

When the soldiers came now it was to hunt for the fugitive Prince Charles Edward, still at large somewhere in the Highlands. If they paused on their way to loot or rape or burn that was merely incidental to their search. After all, Hector told Isobel with that sombre light glowing in his eyes, there was little left for them to take. Great herds of cattle and other livestock had been driven in from the glens to the military post at Fort Augustus, and the soldiers had turned cattle dealers. Buyers came from as far afield as England to stock their farms with the shaggy beasts on which the clans had depended for their prosperity and their lives. When the winter came, said Hector gloomily, the people would starve. Although there was little enough for them to eat even now.

Outside the cave the vibrant green of the leaves on the trees by the river darkened and hung heavy over the water. The short hours of darkness began imperceptibly to lengthen. Isobel realised one day that the spring had gone and it was already summer.

They woke one morning after a warm night to a day of shimmering heat. The sky arched deeply blue overhead, the woods lay silent, as if the birds and animals were too hot to move. Isobel slid from her heather couch, gathered up the plaid which she had discarded some time in the night, and announced that today she would wash their clothes.

Hector sat up and cast a disparaging glance at his own plaid, stiff with dirt so that the colours of the tartan had long been indistinguishable one from another. His shirt was no better: impossible now to tell that it had once been crisply white and ruffled with fine lace.

'I think that would be no bad thing,' he commented with a wry half smile.

He unwound the plaid and pulled off his shirt, casting them at Isobel's feet before skirting the waterfall and plunging deep into the pool. Isobel thought longingly of clear water on warm skin, cooling and cleansing. Like Hector, she would bathe herself as soon as she had washed the clothes.

She began carefully to undress, discarding the soiled gown and petticoat with indescribable relief. It felt strange to be naked again, after so long wearing the same garments day and night. She gathered the heap of clothes into her arms and moved towards the narrow shelf which led under the waterfall. And then she paused, feeling suddenly shy.

She was Hector's wife, and he had seen her naked and known her body in all its intimacy. Yet that had been a long time ago, and the ardent lover of those early days was a stranger now beside the new Hector, aloof and cold and uncaring. She watched him, the black head sleek in its wetness appearing briefly, and then submerging again, followed by the smooth plunging curve of the brown body. He was absorbed in the swim, oblivious to anything else. Very likely he would not even notice her.

She edged her way along the shelf and found a wide flat rock beside the shallower waters of the pool, and crouched there, dropping the clothes in and bending to pummel and squeeze and rub vigorously at the heavy folds of the plaids. It was satisfying to watch the dirt drift away, carried on the little river out between the trees. She worked until even naked as she was the perspiration poured from her body, and the water ran clear at last.

She hung the clothes in the trees nearby, the plaids suddenly brilliant in the sunlight, though the colours had faded a little since she had last seen them clearly. And then she stepped down to the water and edged cautiously into its inviting coolness.

It was delightful, exhilarating, and she became bold, lying down to let the water run over her, plunging her head into it with a gasp of delight, rubbing her long hair clean. Her body looked strangely white and unfamiliar, and far thinner than it had when she had last seen it, but tautened by hard exercise into an unaccustomed litheness.

She splashed happily in the pool until its icy coldness

began to chill her in spite of the sun, and then she pulled herself onto the flat rock, hot to her bare skin, and went to bring her comb from the leather pouch in the cave, and sat in the sunlight pulling the teeth through her wet hair. It was not until she had almost finished that she noticed that Hector had ceased his swimming and was treading water in the pool, watching her through narrowed eyes.

The comb fell unheeded to the rock and she returned his gaze, feeling the colour rise in her face. She was conscious of every smooth firm curve of her own white body, aware as never before of his supple bronzed grace, of the alert pose of his dark head, of the glowing intensity of his eyes. She felt as if every part of her was tingling with life, yet she was utterly still, motionless, waiting.

Then with one smooth silent movement he glided across the pool towards her and emerged in the shallow water at her side. She could not look at him now, hearing his quickened breathing in tune with her own, trembling a little in anticipation.

Then he had her in his arms and was carrying her swiftly along the ledge back to the cave. She felt the spray tingle lightly on her skin as they passed under the fall, felt the coolness of the cave close about her, felt him fling her onto the harsh springy heather of her bed. And with an eager longing cry she reached up to welcome him.

But there, horribly, her joy ended. He took her now as he never had before, urgently, harshly, without one faint trace of tenderness. A few brief painful moments and it was over, and with neither word nor caress he left her, aching and unsatisfied and swept by a desolation more terrible than any she had known until now. When she drew her hands away from where they had moved to hide her face so that he should not see her grief, there was no sign of him. Only her own plaid and the gown and petticoat hung in the sunlight on the trees above the pool.

She did not weep, for the pain was too deep for tears.

If she had ever doubted that he despised and hated her, she knew it now. He had used her to satisfy his need, and the act had been no more significant to him than eating and drinking. Less, perhaps, for she knew how he always ate courteously, with graceful good manners. There had been no such consideration in his taking of her. In the past at least she had known he thought her beautiful, desirable. This time she had been simply a convenient body.

She lay shivering and gazing up at the arching rock of the cave roof, seeing nothing there but his face as she had seen it just now, shadowed, withdrawn. It had been almost as if he had taken her in anger, to punish her for all the disasters which he thought she had brought on him. She knew, horribly, that it had been a rape as brutal as any she had witnessed at Ardshee.

After a time she got up slowly and wandered out of the cave. Her clothes were not quite dry, but they would do: she shrank now from her own nakedness. She dressed quickly, and retreated once more into the cave, and sat on her bed, wondering what to do next. She knew she could not stay here any longer. To be parted from Hector would be infinitely less painful than this, almost as if when he was not there she would not be aware so clearly of the gulf between them.

She examined the contents of her pouch. She retrieved her fallen comb, counted her money—they had not needed to use it—gazed unseeing at the borrowed map, fast disintegrating by now. She did not think any of these things would help her much, but from force of habit she shut them away and fastened the pouch once more beneath her plaid.

She was tempted to set out now, quickly, before Hector returned. But she might well meet him on the way, and that would not do. Besides it would be foolish to set out in broad daylight. Tonight, she thought instead, as soon as it grows dark and Hector is asleep, then I will go. She clasped her hands tightly together in her lap and waited, and her stomach churned with fear, and a weight of grief and despair sat heavy on her heart.

It was already dusk when Hector returned. One glance in his direction told her that his mood was as dark and unyielding as when he had left. He said nothing, only went to his bed and began to wrap his plaid about him for the night. Clearly he had brought no food today.

'We leave at dawn,' he said curtly before lying down. 'The country seems quiet enough to take the risk. I'll go with you as far as I can.'

She was startled out of her immobility. She had not for a moment expected him to reach a decision so close to her own.

Then she had a sudden vision of the main Highland roads crowded with marching soldiers, of the long miles they must cover before she came within reach of her home. And she remembered the other rebels of whom he had spoken, waiting in the crowded fever-ridden jails for the cruel indignity of the gallows. Whatever he had done to her, she could not so certainly tie the noose about Hector's own neck. For in spite of everything she loved him still.

'I can go alone,' she said proudly, matching the coldness of his tone with her own.

'You'd never find your way,' he told her, his contempt only too obvious. 'And if you didn't die of starvation or exposure you'd walk into the first troop of soldiers on the road and suffer rape, or worse.'

She wondered briefly what he would say if she retorted that she had already endured that fate at his hands and did not think the soldiers could do much worse. But instead she only reminded him:

'It is you who are the rebel. Perhaps I would be safer without you.' It sounded ungrateful, but she felt no compunction on that score. She did not think she had much now for which to be grateful.

He gave a snort of derisive laughter.

'*You* safer without me! When if it had not been for you I could be beyond the reach of the soldiers by now—'

'Dead, you mean!' she put in harshly. 'If I'd not been with you you'd have gone chasing after John Campbell and his men would have cut you down where you stood.

I've given you weeks more of life by staying with you—'

'*Dhia*, woman, but you flatter yourself!' His voice was vibrant with scorn. 'Do you think me so inept that I could not dirk a man in the dark and get away with it? I was bred to live like a hunter. If I hadn't had to drag you after me I'd have been a thousand times safer, believe me—'

'Then why did you?' she flung at him, angry tears flooding her eyes. 'I never asked it of you.'

'Why indeed? Well, I will tell you, woman.' He came and stood over her and even in the dark she could see his eyes glowing with bitter fire like his harsh hurried whispered words. 'I drag you with me, Isobel, because I must. You are my fate and my punishment. Because of you John Campbell came again into my life. Because of you he came to Ardshee and the women and children are left weeping and hungry on the shore. Because of you my brother lies dead. Because of you I cannot keep my solemn oath to end my enemy's life. You brought all this on my head, and more, because I was weak enough to be tempted by your wealth and your beauty. And for that one moment of weakness I have paid every day since and shall go on paying until you are gone and John Campbell is dead. But I cannot abandon you, because you are my punishment and I must endure it to the end—' His face loomed close to hers, his voice low and sibilant. 'Now do you see, Isobel? We are bound in pain together until we have paid in full.'

She shrank back, shivering. There was a hint of madness in his words, and yet a cold and deadly logic which was more frightening still, and for a moment almost had her believing he spoke from some deep insight. But she shook her head in denial, though she could find no words to tell him that all he said was untrue, a ghastly nightmare brought on by living too long with horror and pain and grief.

After a moment he drew back, and returned in silence to his bed. She could only just see him in the dark, as he lay down on the heather and turned away from her to sleep.

'We leave at dawn,' was all he said, repeating his order as tonelessly as before. And then he lay still.

Isobel watched him for a long time, as the cave grew darker and his quiet shape merged into the blackness of the night. Slowly her trembling ceased and the bewildered horror his words had awoken in her brain faded, leaving only a lurking shadow tinged with pity. She loved him enough to understand, and to forgive. She could only hope that one day he would be able to put all these terrible things behind him, the horrors of the battle and the attack on Ardshee, of Hugh's death and the long flight. Then perhaps he would be able to forgive her too.

She sat on her bed thinking and planning for perhaps an hour, until she was sure he was asleep. She could no longer see him, but she crossed the cave and gently, very softly, laid her mouth on his hair, warm and dense and springing under her lips. And then she turned away and crept beneath the grey roaring curtain of the fall and set out along the narrow ledge into the waiting darkness of the trees.

CHAPTER
NINETEEN

FOR a moment when she opened her eyes Isobel expected to see the warm rose-coloured hangings of her bed at home, lit by the firelight glowing in the dusk. Those had been the soothing familiar surroundings which had met her gaze when she had woken after that last illness—or was this perhaps the same illness, and she had only dozed to wake again after a succession of hideous nightmares?

But then her eyes rested on rough-hewn stones, moss-grown, an earth floor, a crudely-made door, and she felt a moment of bewildered panic. Where in God's name was she? What had happened to bring her here?

And then, slowly, painfully, she remembered. Not that remembering answered her questions, for there was nothing remotely familiar about the rough stone hut in which she lay, lulled by the distant sound of running water—a small burn perhaps. And there was nothing to tell her what had brought her here.

But she did remember her return to Ardshee, the long flight, the fear of discovery. And Hector, angry, hate-filled, accusing. Hector who would never love her now. And so she had run from him, though without him she could never hope for happiness or completion; and wandered lost in the mountains until sickness and exhaustion had overcome her at last.

He had haunted her fever. She had seen his face constantly in those nightmarish visions, the face of Hector the arrogant young chieftain in her garden, assured and proud, the face of Hector as she had seen him last, wild, bearded, desperate. That face had come to her most, and sometimes it had seemed full of an unaccustomed tenderness, and she had thought his voice spoke caressingly, calling her name. But always there was that gulf between them and she could not reach him. And now even that vision had gone, with the fever and pain which had left her weak and weary and wondering where she was.

It was clear, she realised, as she turned her head to look about the room, that she had not come here by herself, and that someone—perhaps whoever had brought her here—had been caring for her. She wore only her petticoat, and the plaid was wrapped about her, to keep her warm and protect her thin body from the harshness of the heather and bracken which formed her bed. Nearby, on the floor, lay a small wooden bowl, half-filled with water, and further off the embers of a fire still held a red glow in the dim light. She could see her blue gown, torn and faded now, folded carefully on a rock set like a stool beside the wall.

The hut was low-ceilinged, scarcely high enough for a man to stand upright indoors, and it had no windows. What light there was slid between the uneven boulders of which it was made, or around the ill-fitting door. The daylight seemed very bright, but that must be because of the dimness or her own weak state, for she could hear rain pattering on the decaying thatch, and in one place the water dripped steadily through and spread a muddy puddle on the floor.

Perhaps it was because of the rain that she did not know anyone was coming until the door was jerked open—clearly it would not open any other way—and a dark figure appeared outlined against the grey daylight. Not tall—his head only bent a little under the broad lintel—but slender, graceful, barefooted and dressed in the everyday belted plaid of the Highlander, his hair a wild silhouette about his head. With eyes closed, she thought, I would know him, for however little he feels for me he is in my blood and my bones for ever. Her heart quickened painfully.

'Hector,' she whispered, and it was at once a statement, a question, a plea.

In a moment the door was pushed to and he was at her

side, kneeling in the dust, and his long cool fingers were smoothing her forehead, stroking her hair with unmistakable tenderness.

'So you have woken, my heart.' His voice came to her soft as a breeze, warm and caressing as the voice in her dreams.

Perhaps, she thought, this is a dream, and I am not awake after all. She dared not speak, for fear that she might break the spell, or wake to find that it was all an illusion. She only smiled and lay quietly, wrapped in unutterable contentment, feeling his hands lingeringly gentle as he brought her water or broth or milk, as he smoothed the plaid about her or brushed the hair from her eyes or bathed her face and hands. He said little, but his dark eyes held a light she had never seen in them before, warm yet untroubled, full of tender concern.

For two days she slept and woke and slept again and always he was there, watching over her, caring for her, demanding nothing from her but that she should grow well. She began, very slowly, almost as if holding her breath in fear, to believe that this new Hector was no illusion, but the man she loved grown suddenly, inexplicably, loving. When she opened her eyes one morning and felt new strength in her limbs she turned to where he lay stretched on the heather at her side, deeply asleep, and dared to put out a hand to touch his hair.

He stirred, as if even in sleep he was alert to her every need, and his eyes opened to meet hers. For a long moment they gazed at her, those long-fringed eyes, dark and deep and full of some emotion she could not read. Or dared not, for fear she might be wrong. Instead she smiled, but there was no answering smile.

'Can you ever bring yourself to forgive me for what I did to you?' he asked suddenly in a whisper. She saw that he feared her answer, and laid her hand over his.

'What do you want me to forgive?' she returned gently, but teasing a little. Yet there was so much which had come between them that she had to know.

'Everything,' he said simply. He turned his hand

beneath hers and imprisoned it, carrying it to his lips. He was not looking at her. 'I do not think I could forgive anyone for using me as I used you,' he went on, deeply serious. 'I can only hope that you are more forgiving than I am myself. You see, Isobel, I blamed you for all the things which had happened, because I could not bear to blame myself. It was I who brought disaster on my people, by leading them to a war which was not of their choosing. Oh, I know they would have come all the same, for love of the fight; but I should have known where it would end. And because I did not count the cost nearly a hundred men will never go home to Ardshee, and nothing will ever be the same again. You had only a small part to play in that, and even then I was to blame that you came into the story at all—' Suddenly he looked at her again. 'Though I still do not know why you came back.'

'Because I love you, of course,' she told him after a little pause.

She heard the sharp astonished intake of breath, saw the colour drain from his face and then flood it again, felt his fingers tighten about hers.

'You . . . you love . . . me . . . ?' he breathed, and she nodded, smiling a little, holding her breath as an incredible realisation began to grow within her. 'After all I did to you—all I said—' he went on.

'Before,' she corrected him. 'Long before. Always, I think, if I had only known it. That is why there is no need to forgive, because I understand.'

He bent his head again, and she could no longer see his face. She gazed at the top of his head, the dark springing hair, and tried to guess what he was thinking.

'Then,' he broke out at last, his voice muffled because his lips were pressed hard against her hand, 'then I am blessed beyond words—'

And all at once he had her in his arms and was kissing her with all the sweetness and tenderness of which she had dreamed, but without passion because she had been so ill.

'Oh, my heart,' he murmured, as she nestled close,

her head against his shoulder, 'I feared I was too late—
that I'd lost all hope of you for ever. For I think like you I
have loved from the first and only knew it when you had
gone. God knows I do not deserve—' But she silenced
him with a kiss.

There was no need for words for a long time after that.
When at last they did draw apart to gaze at each other,
laughing gently with joy and wonder, he told her, in
fragmented phrases lost between kisses, how he had
woken in the cave to find 'her gone, and remorse had
swept him that he had driven her to this. And then he
had set out to find her.

She had covered her tracks well, and he had wandered
helplessly, asking at cottages if she had been seen,
searching every glen, every settlement for signs of her.
And only come on her at last, collapsed in delirium,
when he had almost given up hope of finding her. And
then, of course, he had feared that she would die before
he could tell her how he loved her and beg her forgive-
ness.

'Where are we now?' she asked him. 'Had I walked
far?'

He shook his head.

'We are in Ardnamurchan where we began. I think
you had been wandering in circles for days.' A sparkle of
excitement lit his eyes. 'I was forgetting, Isobel—the
news—I thought it could mean nothing to us, with you so
ill, but now—! There are French ships, not far from here
so they say. If we can make our way to Moidart—but it
must be soon, in the next day or two—' He broke off,
suddenly doubtful. 'But perhaps you wish to go back to
your parents. You said so once.'

'Only because you wanted it,' she replied. 'Where you
go, my love, then I will go too. I shall be well enough to
come. I think I am so happy I could do anything—' And
he drew her closer to kiss her again.

Later he left her briefly to light the little fire and bake
bannocks over it for them to eat. He had become quite a
beggar these days, he told her smiling, calling at this

house and that for meal and milk and anything else they could give.

'I hope you were careful,' she said, briefly serious, but he grinned.

'For you I would take any risk—but I am afraid of nothing any more. I know in my heart that all will be well.'

Isobel sat up when he brought her the food and ate hungrily, and it might have been a sumptuous feast for the happiness with which they shared it. Afterwards she slept a little in his arms; and woke to the delirious joy of finding him there and knowing that his love of her was a reality. He smiled as she opened her eyes, the sweet warm youthful smile which was so new to her and which, even weak as she was, set her pulses racing.

He brought her milk to drink, and then set to work to comb her hair for her, matted and tangled as it was after the long illness. He worked slowly, because he was anxious not to hurt her, and she sat half-leaning against him, enjoying his nearness and the caressing touch on her hair.

'What became of your ship?' she asked dreamily, as her mind lingered on his news of those other ships waiting off the coast.

'Oh, she was lost long since, I imagine,' he said. 'We left her when we joined the Prince, and I've not thought of her since. We shall have a grander ship to take us to France, you can be sure.'

She smiled, and he paused to kiss her briefly before continuing his loving task. He had almost finished when a small unexpected sound caused Isobel to raise her head, listening hard.

There was silence, but for the rain and the chatter of the burn. And then it came again, clear and unmistakable. She glanced at Hector, and knew he heard it too.

'Someone's outside,' she whispered, and shivered. He put his arms about her, his mouth on her hair.

'An animal perhaps,' he suggested soothingly.

But at that moment a voice spoke just beyond the door, quietly, but with authority and in English.

'Yes, you are quite right,' it said. 'There is someone in there. Bring up the others.'

Isobel thought she would hear that voice for ever in her nightmares.

'John Campbell!' she mouthed despairingly.

Suddenly brisk and practical Hector brought her the faded gown.

'Dress quickly—I'm going to have a look.'

As she obeyed he crept to the side of the hut and put his eye to the widest gap near the door. Even from here she could see the gleam of scarlet outside. She was pulling the plaid about her when he came back to her, and he helped her, saying softly:

'Yes, it is John Campbell, and he is alone. You must be ready to leave at once, when I say—'

'But how can we?' she whispered in anguish. 'He is just by the door. He will be armed. We can't escape.'

'I am going to kill him.'

She shook her head in unbelieving dismay, struggling to find her voice.

'He will be watching the door. He will kill you—and you heard what he said. The soldiers are coming. Even if you kill him—' He laid a finger over her mouth, his expression implacable.

'I shall kill him,' he repeated.

He knelt suddenly at her side and drew his dirk, and she heard him murmur some kind of prayer.

'Holy Michael, give strength to my arm. Holy Mary defend me. Jesus stay by me—'

And then he paused only to kiss her once on the forehead and strode to the door, flinging it wide.

'John Campbell!' he cried. 'I am ready for you!'

Isobel dragged herself from the bed and stumbled to the door, sinking down on the threshold. She saw John draw his sword and face Hector along its length, a little smile tilting his mouth, as eager as a lover going to a tryst. For long seconds they circled each other, like wild cats with their prey, the two blades poised, unequal, gleaming in the rain, their eyes watchful, alert, the only sound their feet light on the grass.

And then Hector lunged forward beneath the long blade and John grasped his wrist and they were suddenly still, grappling silently, their eyes raised to that shorter blade held in the lean brown hand, the point turned towards John's heart.

John's grasp tightened, he bent and twisted the wrist, forcing it backwards, all his will directed to loosening that deadly hold. The fingers on the dirk moved, splayed a little and closed again, locked white about the dark ornate leather, thrusting back against the clawing hold on the wrist. The upraised arms quivered, poised over the two men and between them, moving neither one way nor the other. At his other side John's free arm drew back, slowly bringing the point of the sword steadily within reach of Hector's straining body.

And then Hector made a sudden sideways movement. A sharp twist of the wrist, and his blade thrust downwards and found its mark. The sword fell useless to the ground. John lurched into Hector's arms, his eyes momentarily wide and startled. And then he too fell and lay still.

His face expressionless Hector rolled him onto his back and straightened his limbs and closed his eyes. And then he wiped the dirk clean on the wet grass and held out his arm to Isobel.

'Come,' he said. She ran trembling to him and his arm closed about her. For a moment he paused, holding her, yet gazing sombrely down at the dead man. She wondered if he too had seen the pistol John had carried thrust into his belt, but had not used though it might have saved him. He drew her closer, and then on a sudden impulse bent down and broke off a sprig from a plant of bog myrtle growing near his foot, and laid it on John's chest, tucked beneath the white belt which crossed it.

'Why do you do that?' asked Isobel.

'It is the badge of his clan. He was a Highlander after all.' It sounded almost like a tribute.

His arm tightened briefly about her.

'It is over,' he said. 'Let us go.'

'Is that . . . is that really the end? Or will there
be others of his family . . . ?' She had learned too well
the relentlessness of the Highland memory for past
wrongs.

'There is no one who will weep for him,' Hector told
her, and she felt a sudden surge of pity for the dead man.
But it could not last long. There was no time now for
pity.

Up the winding track from the glen below the hut
came a scarlet file of men, moving closer every minute.
And it was at that moment that her legs gave way and
Isobel sank weakly to the ground.

'Hector, I can't—' she faltered, tears rushing to her
eyes. But without a moment's hesitation he bent and
raised her in his arms.

'I'll carry you, my heart.'

He strode along the path away from the hut and the
approaching soldiers, but she struggled to free herself
and cried out:

'Leave me, Hector—we will never escape like this.
You will be better off without me.'

'Never!' he silenced her, his grasp tightening about
her. 'Without you there is nothing.' And she knew she
could not move him. She placed her arms about his neck
and held tight and he carried her on, at a brisk steady
walk which she knew would be useless if the soldiers
once set out in pursuit.

Over his shoulder she saw that the head of the file had
reached the hut. There was a shout, and the first man
gestured wildly as the others came running. They
gathered about the body, stooping to examine it. And
then they began to look about them.

It was only a moment before they had seen the
fugitives and came streaming along the track behind
them. Hector's pace quickened, though already he was
breathless with the weight of his burden.

'I'll have to carry you across my shoulder,' he gasped
at last, apologetically, and paused to shift her into that
ignominious position. It was not very comfortable, but
he could move faster like that, breaking into a run which

for the time being at least lengthened the distance
between them and the soldiers.

The path dropped gently down and then rose again
steeply onto a bare rocky hillside. The rain seeped
through her plaid, and Isobel began to shiver. She
longed for the abandoned bed, but she said nothing. She
could hear the running feet of the soldiers clattering on
the rocks as they came nearer.

Hector stumbled and then righted himself, but he was
labouring now, and she sensed that every ounce of
energy and will power was concentrated on forcing one
step to follow another, doggedly, stubbornly, up the
slope. His pace had slowed again to little more than a
walk.

When the path levelled out he gathered speed again
for a while, and then the track rounded a bend and
descended once more, treacherous with loose stones,
into a small glen. Hector's feet slid uncomfortably on the
stones, their customary sureness lost in exhaustion. His
breathing came now in sobbing gasps, and she could feel
his hold on her slackening.

At a small stone bridge crossing a swift-flowing burn
he halted, setting her on the parapet, and bent his head.

'I cannot . . .' he gasped. '. . . I am sorry . . . but I
cannot do it . . .'

She glanced to where the soldiers were running down
that dangerous path towards them. A hundred yards
perhaps, at most—

'Leave me!' she implored him. 'Hector, my darling,
leave me. At least you will be safe, and I do not think
they will kill me.'

He shook his head, unable to speak. She could see
how his hands trembled as they rested on the stonework
to either side of her.

A shot rang out and hit the parapet, scattering small
splinters of stone around them.

'Please, Hector!'

He made a great effort and drew himself up, and lifted
her again over his shoulder. And then he set out once
more at a swaying stumbling run which she knew would

only delay their capture a little longer. Another shot just missed them, and then another, closer still.

And then she heard Hector give some kind of grunted exclamation, and he veered off the track, his pace gaining new momentum.

A few yards more, and she was aware that he had run under some kind of stone archway and they were in a paved yard surrounded by outbuildings. He ran into the nearest open doorway and there set her down, reaching out for support towards a wooden upright.

It was a stable with a hayloft above and one or two horses in their stalls, an oddly prosperous-looking place for the Highlands. And facing them, his face blank with astonishment, was a man leaning on a broom.

Hector, too breathless to speak, made an appealing gesture with his hands. For what seemed an age the man looked from one to the other and back again, considering, his face showing neither welcome nor suspicion. Then he flung the broom aside and went to the furthest stall and led out the nervous grey horse which stood there.

'In there!' he said in Gaelic, nodding towards the stall. 'Under the manger.'

Hector pulled Isobel after him and flung himself into the stall. They huddled together beneath the wooden manger, half-concealed by pungent straw, and watched as the man returned the horse to his place. He had just resumed his sweeping when the soldiers reached the door.

'Where did they go?' demanded a curt English voice.

The sweeping ceased briefly, and then continued, though no answer was given.

'Search the whole place,' came the next order. 'Run your bayonets into the hay.' Isobel clasped Hector tightly, and he drew her head against his breast and rested his mouth on her hair. He was making a superhuman effort to control his breathing so that he should not give them away, and she could feel how much he trembled still after his long exertion. His heart throbbed fiercely beneath her cheek.

They heard the soldiers tramping about the barn, and
in the hayloft overhead, and the sound of steel thrust
into the hay set Isobel's teeth on edge. If they had chosen
that hiding place, she thought, and shuddered.

Steps came nearer, and the sweeping stopped again.

'I would not be at going near that horse, if I wass you,'
came the man's sing-song voice, in English this time. 'It
iss he that iss the ill-tempered beast.'

They heard the soldier hesitate, and then say,

'I'll take a look all the same.'

Beneath the horse Isobel could see his feet coming
into view, neat in their buckled shoes, and the white
gaiters above. They stepped nearer, and the horse
swung sideways, snorting, his hooves moving restlessly
on the straw. She could not see any more of the man
beyond his feet, but she sensed that his eyes ran over the
horse and the manger and the scattered straw. He stood
there for what seemed an interminably long time. It was
growing late now, and it was already dark beneath the
manger, and the horse was large and restless; but Hector
had killed their Captain, and the soldiers would move
heaven and earth to find him.

'They must be in here somewhere, I'm sure of it,'
came the soldier's voice, and the feet moved away. If she
had dared to make a sound Isobel would have wept with
relief.

'Keep an eye on this place, Private Hopper, and we'll
search next door. Keep your wits about you now.'

The soldiers tramped out again, and their friend went
on with his sweeping, whistling faintly between his teeth.
Distant thuds and shouts told them where the soldiers
were searching now.

Night fell outside, and at the far end of the stable a
lantern was lit, sending long beams to blacken the
shadow beneath the manger. It was warm and still and
Isobel began to feel drowsy. The noise of searching
moved away and then drew nearer again, on the other
side of the stable. And then orders were shouted, feet
tramped noisily on the flagstones, and silence fell at last.

The man shuffled through the straw to where they lay.

'They've set up camp just outside the gate,' he whispered. 'It's dark now, but there's a guard by the door.'

Hector struggled to his feet, gently raising Isobel to stand beside him.

'God will reward you for this,' he said to the man. And then: 'We'll go now.' He put his arm about Isobel. 'It's our only hope,' he whispered into her ear. 'If we stay till daylight they'll find us.'

They crept to the door and he peered round it. The lantern light spilled onto the flags, just reaching the scarlet-coated figure who stood there, his hands resting on his musket. The man in the stable laid his hand briefly on Hector's arm, signing to him to remain where he was, and then wandered across the yard, pausing to speak to the soldier, keeping him talking with his back towards them.

Hector turned sharply and lifted Isobel, and then slipped soft-footed into the yard, sliding as soon as he could into the shadows at its edge. The stable hand was talking loudly now, with extravagant gestures, and the soldier was laughing appreciatively. Hector reached the archway and darted beneath it.

Outside, a camp fire glowed, and the voices of the soldiers reached them on the damp still air. Hector turned from it to skirt the side of the stable buildings and the house beyond, and then broke into a run. The friendly blackness of the night swallowed them up.

They did not rest until they knew they had left house and soldiers far behind them.

Three days later Hector and Isobel came at evening to a wide shining sea loch set in a tumbled landscape of rock and mountain. The last lingering fires of sunset touched the sea with rose, and the peaks about it, and lingered on the tall masts and graceful lines of the two ships rocking at anchor on the still waters of the loch. On the shore a knot of men waited, black against the white sand. Beside them a small rowing boat was drawn up, and they were clearly making ready to use it.

Hector paused, his arm about Isobel, gazing at the

scene. They had come here by slow stages, resting often
so that Isobel could harbour her small strength. Just now
they had identified themselves to the Highlanders on
watch in the surrounding hills and been allowed to pass.
Their journey was nearly over.

Hector slid his arm down to take Isobel's hand in his
and lead her to the shore.

The waiting fugitives—several of them leaders of the
fated rebel army—welcomed them warmly. After a
bewildering few moments—for she had grown unused to
company—Isobel found herself standing before a tall
young man wearing a motley assortment of tartan
clothes with light auburn hair roughly tied back and an
unkempt red beard. Brown eyes met her gaze and he
smiled: it was a smile of considerable charm.

'You are welcome, Mrs MacLean,' he said in heavily-
accented English. But the accent, she knew, was not
Highland, nor even Scots.

And then, with alarm and confusion, she knew who he
was, and sank, blushing furiously, into a deep curtsey.
She knelt now before the man who above all should
carry the burden of guilt for the suffering land he was
leaving: Charles Edward Stewart, the Young Pretender,
his long flight ended at last.

Late in the night Isobel stirred and woke from a brief but
restful sleep, and lay listening to the sounds of wind and
waves and rigging, revelling in the unaccustomed comfort of the bunk on which she lay. *L'Heureux* they called
this ship, Hector had told her, 'the Fortunate One'. It
could not be better named, she thought, though she
knew that for Hector this moment of parting must be
hard indeed.

He had left her soon after they came aboard, so that
she could rest while he went to talk to the other fugitives,
to grieve with them for the cause which was lost and for
the ruin which had come upon their people because of it.
And also, she knew, to stand on the deck and gaze his
last on the land he loved and might never see again.

Distantly she heard the sailors calling orders to each

other in French. Another language to learn, another strange land to grow to understand at the journey's end. But this time she would not be alone.

Hector came to her at last, as the first dawn light crept into the cabin. For a moment she scarcely recognised him, for he had shaved off his beard. And she saw that the young man from the orchard had gone for ever. The man who came now to kneel at her side and draw her into his arms was older and leaner, darkly tanned, with new lines etched about his mouth, and a new bitter knowledge deep in his eyes.

And he loved her.

She reached out and slid her arms about his neck, and made room for him to lie at her side, raising her mouth to meet his kiss, firm and warm and tender. The ship rolled gently through the morning mist, leaving behind the mountains and lochs and glens and the treeless wind-swept islands. Somewhere, hundreds of miles away, the coast of France waited, silent beneath the same veiled sky, to welcome the fugitives to safety and a new life.

A long road lay ahead of them, with its share of hardship and sadness and pain, but in Hector's arms Isobel MacLean was smiling and unafraid. For she had come home at last.

Your chance to step into the past and re-live four love stories...

TAKE FOUR BOOKS FREE

An introduction to
The Masquerade Reader Service.

NO OBLIGATION.

HISTORICAL ROMANCES